YAN LIANKE

Yan Lianke was born in 1958 in Henan Province, China. He is the author of numerous novels and short-story collections, including *Serve the People!*, *Dream of Ding Village*, *Lenin's Kisses* and *The Four Books*. He has been awarded the Hua Zhong World Chinese Literature Prize, the Lao She Liverary Award and the Franz Kafka Prize, whose previous winners include Václav Havel, John Banville and Harold Pinter. He has also been shortlisted for an array of prizes including the Man Booker International Prize, the Independent Foreign Fiction Prize and the Prix Femina Etranger. He currently lives and writes in Beijing.

YAN LIANKE

The Years, Months, Days

TRANSLATED FROM THE CHINESE BY
Carlos Rojas

VINTAGE

1 3 5 7 9 10 8 6 4 2

Vintage
20 Vauxhall Bridge Road,
London SW1V 2SA

Vintage is part of the Penguin Random House group of companies
whose addresses can be found at global.penguinrandomhouse.com

Penguin
Random House
UK

First published in Vintage in 2018
First published in the USA by Grove Atlantic in 2017
First published in China as *Nian yue ri* by *Harvest* magazine in 1997

penguin.co.uk/vintage

A CIP catalogue record for this book is available from the British Library

ISBN 9781529115741

Printed and bound in Great Britain by Clays Ltd, Elcograf S.p.A.

Penguin Random House is committed to a sustainable future
for our business, our readers and our planet. This book is made
from Forest Stewardship Council® certified paper.

MIX
Paper | Supporting
responsible forestry
FSC® C018179

Translator's Preface

He kept talking to the dog until it became quite used to the sound of his voice. It hardly looked up now when he spoke. It came and went without trepidation, eating and barking its curt acknowledgement from across the street. Soon now, Neville told himself, I'll be able to pat his head. The days passed into pleasant weeks, each hour bringing him closer to a companion.

Richard Matheson, I Am Legend

We may approach Yan Lianke's 1997 novella *The Years, Months, Days* through another, perhaps rather unexpected, work – Richard Matheson's iconic 1954 novel,

I Am Legend. The protagonist of the latter work, Robert Neville, finds himself in a post-apocalyptic world in which humanity has been ravaged by a virulent bacillus. Neville believes he may be the only survivor of this plague. One day he finds a stray dog, and – desperate for any form of companionship – attempts to befriend it. Although the dog is also traumatized by the plague, Neville succeeds in gaining its trust, and the dog becomes the most important being in his life.

Yan Lianke's novella is set against a similarly apocalyptic landscape. Following a devastating drought, the entire population of a remote Henan village flees, leaving behind only an old man and a stray dog. The old man refuses to follow the others because he doubts that he could survive the journey, while the dog stays because it is blind – its eyes were scorched by the sun when the villagers attempted to sacrifice it to the rain gods. Alone in the deserted village, the old man and the blind dog develop a close bond as they battle starvation. The old man perceives not only the dog but also other animals and plants as either helping him survive, or attempting to take advantage of him. Acute hunger leads the old man to view the entire world in his own image, and simultaneously to see it as his mortal enemy.

Famine was a fact of life in the poor rural community in which Yan Lianke grew up. Yan was born in 1958, the first year of the Great Leap Forward – a political campaign that was intended to jumpstart China's economy but instead precipitated the Great Famine, in which tens of millions of Chinese starved to death in a three-year period. Yan used this historic famine as the backdrop of his 2011 novel, *The Four Books*. Other works also focus on remote rural communities facing environmental and existential challenges: *Streams of Time* (1998) features a village poisoned by industrial contaminants (a version of what came to be known as cancer villages), where all the residents succumb to esophageal cancer before they reach the age of forty; in *Lenin's Kisses* (2004), almost all the residents of the village are handicapped or disabled; *Dream of Ding Village* (2006) depicts an AIDS village in Yan's home province of Henan (which was the epicenter of China's 1990s rural AIDS epidemic). What distinguishes *The Years, Months, Days* from these works, however, is that the focus is not on a community, but rather on an individual who finds himself almost completely isolated.

As in many of Yan's other works, in *The Years, Months, Days* the author does not use quotation marks to differentiate dialogue from narrative. Instead, each of the old man's utterances – whether he is speaking to another person, to an animal, a plant, or to himself – opens with a pair of dashes and ends with a line break, or segues back to the main narrative. In order to preserve this sense of continuity between narrative and dialogue, this English translation of the work uses quotation marks only for the handful of passages in which people are talking to one another, and uses italics for all other remarks by the protagonist to his non-human surroundings, or to himself. The intended result is to help blur the boundary – at a typographical and a conceptual level – between the protagonist's consciousness and his immediate environment.

Yan Lianke's own relationship with his community and with the outside world is a complicated one. Several of his works have been banned, recalled, or self-censored within China due to the perception that their contents are politically sensitive – even as many of those same works have won prestigious accolades abroad. Yan has, for example, repeatedly explained that he felt he had to preemptively censor himself while writing *Dream of Ding Village*, so that the novel would be accepted by the censors. In the end the work was published, but was banned after the first printing. It went on to be shortlisted for the *Independent* Foreign Fiction Prize. *The Four Books* was not accepted for publication by any Mainland publisher either, but was published in Taiwan and went on to be shortlisted for the Man Booker International Prize. Most recently, his novel *The Day the Sun Died* (2015) also failed to be accepted by any Mainland publishers, but was published in Taiwan and won Hong Kong's top literary award, the Dream of the Red Chamber Prize. *The Years, Months, Days* won Mainland China's triannual Lu Xun Literary Prize in 2001, and remains one of his best-known works in his home country.

I Am Legend famously concludes with Neville coming to perceive himself from a previously unthinkable perspective. The end of *The Years, Months, Days* gestures to a similar reversal – pulling the reader out of the old man's focus on his own survival, and offering a hint that his memory might become the stuff of legend.

Carlos Rojas

THE YEARS, MONTHS, DAYS

In the year of the great drought, time was baked to ash; and if you tried to grab the sun, it would stick to your palm like charcoal. One sun after another passed over-head, and from dawn till dusk, the Elder could hear his own hair burning. Occasionally he would reach up to the sky, and could smell the stench of burned fingernails. *Damn this sky!* He always cursed this way as he emerged from the empty village and stepped into the intermi-nable loneliness. He peered side-eyed at the sun, then announced, *Blindy, let's go.* His blind dog followed his faint footsteps, and like a pair of shadows they left the village.

The Elder climbed the mountain, stomping the sun-light under his feet. The rays of light shining down from the eastern ridge pounded his face, his hands, and his feet like bamboo canes. His face was burning as though it had been slapped, and as the corners of his eyes met the deep wrinkles on his cheeks, the fiery red pain seemed to conceal countless pearls like glowing embers.

The Elder went to take a piss.

The blind dog followed him.

For half a month, the first thing the Elder and the dog would do every morning after they woke up was to go to Baliban Hill, to take a piss. On the side of the hill facing the sun, there was a corn seedling the Elder had planted. There was only this single seedling, standing alone in the middle of this devastating drought – and under the searing sun it appeared so green that it was as though the color were dripping off it. When the seedling lacked water, it relied on the Elder's and the dog's urine that had accumulated overnight. The Elder saw that the seedling appeared to have grown another three fingers taller since the day before, and where it had previously only had four leaves, now it had five. His heart started pounding and he felt a surge of warmth in his chest, as a smile rippled across his face. The seedling grew only one leaf at a time, and the Elder wondered why scholar trees, elm trees, and toon trees all grew two leaves at a time?

The Elder turned to his blind dog and asked, *Why is it that the leaves of trees and crops grow differently?* He gazed at the dog's head and then, without waiting for the dog to answer, he turned and left, continuing to reflect as he walked away. The Elder looked up, held his hand to his forehead, and traced the sun's rays. In the distance, he saw the bare mountain ridge glistening purple, as though there were a thick layer of smoke on the ground. The Elder knew this was nighttime air being released from the soil by the heat of the sun.

The villagers had all resolved to flee. As a result of the drought, the wheat in the fields had died, the mountain peaks had been left barren, and the entire world had withered. The daily hopes of the villagers had also dried up. The drought had continued until the autumn sowing season, when suddenly there was a downpour and the streets were filled with the sound of pounding drums. Everyone had been shouting, 'Autumn sowing . . . autumn sowing! Heaven has given us an autumn sowing season!' Adults shouted, children shouted, men shouted, and women shouted as though they were performing in an opera – their delighted voices flowed down the streets of the village, from east to west, from west to east, and then from the village over to the mountain ridge.

'It's autumn sowing season.'

'It's autumn sowing season.'

'Heaven has given us rain, to let us proceed with the autumn sowing.'

These shouts, by both young and old, shook the entire mountain range. Sparrows that had alighted on tree branches were startled from their perches and flew away, their feathers drifting down like snow. Chickens and pigs stood astonished in the doorways of houses, their faces pale with shock. The oxen in cattle sheds suddenly started tugging at the ropes tied to their snouts, as their nostrils were ripped open and dark blood flowed into the feed troughs. All the cats and dogs crawled up onto the roofs of houses and gazed down at the villagers in terror.

For three days in a row, clouds grew increasingly dense.

Everyone from Liujiajian Village, Wujiahe Village, Qianliang Village, Houliang Village, Shuanmazhuang Village – in short, everyone from the entire Balou Mountain region – took the corn seed they had stored and rushed to sow their fields.

Three days later, the clouds dispersed, and the searing sun once again bore down on the mountain ridge like a fire.

Six months later, half of the villagers locked their doors and courtyard gates, and fled the drought. Over the next three days and two nights, a steady stream of refugees fled. The crowd of refugees grew like ants relocating to another anthill, as they surged along the road behind the village, heading out into the world. The sound of their footsteps echoed back to the village, pounding on the doors and windows of every house.

The Elder had been one of the last to decide to leave. That was the ninth day of the sixth lunar month, and the Elder gathered with a group of several dozen other villagers. The villagers asked, 'Where should we go?' The Elder replied, 'Let's go east.' The villagers said, 'What is in the east?' The Elder replied that east was the direction of Xuzhou, and in three to ten days they could make it there and live comfortably. They all headed east. The burning sun pounded the mountain road and plumes of dust rose every time they took a step. When they reached Baliban Field, however, the Elder stopped. He went and peed behind his field, then returned and told the other villagers, 'You should go on. Continue heading east.'

'What about you?'

'A corn plant has sprouted in my field.'

'Will a single corn plant keep you from starving, Elder?'

'I'm seventy-two years old, and would surely die of exhaustion if I tried to walk for three days. If I'm going to die either way, I'd prefer to die in my own village.'

The other villagers left. They drifted away like a dark mass, and under the searing sun they disappeared into a cloud of dust. The Elder stood at the end of his field until they vanished from sight, at which point a feeling of solitude struck his heart with a thud. His entire body began to tremble, as he suddenly realized that he, a seventy-two-year-old man, was now the only living soul in the entire village – and perhaps even the entire mountain range. There was a vast emptiness in his heart, as a sense of stillness and desolation enveloped his body.

On that morning, as the sun was changing from yellow to red as it passed over the eastern mountains, the Elder and his dog had gone out to Baliban Field as usual. From a distance, the Elder saw that in the center of this field, the corn seedling – which was already as tall as a chopstick – appeared as green as a drop of water under the red sun. He turned and asked the blind dog, *Can you smell it?* Then added, *It's so fragrant, you can smell it from countless li away.* The blind dog angled its head up to him, rubbed his leg, then silently ran over to the seedling.

Ahead of them was a deep gully, from which trapped heat surged out and singed the Elder's cheeks. The Elder removed his white shirt, rolled it into a ball, and wiped his face. He could smell the reek of sweat three to five inches deep. *This would make excellent fertilizer,* he thought. *I'll let this seedling grow for another month, then I'll wash my shirt, bring the waste water to the field, and let the seedling enjoy it as though it were a New Year's feast.* The Elder held his shirt under his armpits, like a precious treasure. The seedling appeared before him. It was one palm tall, had five leaves, but had not yet produced the bud the Elder was hoping for. He examined the top of the seedling, brushing away some dust as a feeling of disappointment welled up in his heart.

The dog rubbed against the Elder's leg. It walked once around the seedling, then again. The Elder said, *Blindy, go away.* The dog stopped and barked several times like a dried tangerine peel, then lifted its head toward the Elder, as though there were something it urgently had to do.

The Elder knew that the dog needed to pee. He went over to an old scholar tree and fetched his hoe – the Elder always hung his tools there when he wasn't using them – then went back and dug a small hole on the west side of the seedling – the previous day it had been the east side. He told the dog, *OK, go ahead and pee.*

Before the Elder could check to see if the dog had finished urinating, the seventy-two-year-old man's eyes were struck by something. His eyes hurt, his heart began to pound, when he saw that the seedling's lowest two leaves had developed some tiny black dots, as though they were covered in tiny wheat grain shells. *Are these dry spots? Each morning I come to pee and each evening I bring the seedling water. How could it be suffering from dryness?* Just as he was standing up again, the dog's yellow urine struck his head. It occurred to him that those dots were not a result of dryness, but rather were an indication that the fertilizer was too strong. Dog urine is much fattier than human urine, and also much warmer. The Elder complained, *Blindy, I'll fuck your ancestors, yet you still insist on peeing.* He lashed out with his foot and violently kicked the dog, which landed several feet away like a sack of millet. *I told you to pee,* the Elder shouted, *but you deliberately tried to burn the seedling, didn't you?*

The dog stood there, its well-like eye sockets staring blankly.

The Elder said, *Serves you right.* With an angry glance, he squatted down, held the tender leaves, and carefully inspected the black dots on their jade-like surface. He quickly reached over and grabbed some white foam from the dog's urine, which had not yet been fully absorbed by the soil, and tossed it away. Next he used his hoe to refill the hole with several handfuls of the urine-mud, then said to the dog, *Let's go. Let's go fetch some water. If we don't get water to dilute this fertilizer, in less than two days the seedling will have burned up.*

The dog continued along the original path toward the mountain ridge, and the Elder followed it – his footsteps sounding like withered leaves landing under the hot sun. However, the seedling's crisis resembled the Elder's and the dog's footsteps – it followed them away, then followed them back.

After the seedling's sixth leaf appeared, the Elder went to fetch some water, but as he was on his way to the well a sudden breeze blew off his straw hat. The hat rolled down the street, and the Elder ran after it.

That breeze started off slow, then gradually picked up speed, forming a little twister. As a result, the hat always remained a foot ahead of the Elder, who chased it all the way to the village entrance. Several times he just barely managed to touch the hat, but the twister always pulled it away again. The Elder was seventy-two years old, and his legs were not as strong as before. He thought to himself, *I don't even want this hat anymore. How about that? I'm the only person left in this entire village. I could easily go into anyone's house and find myself another one.* The Elder looked up, and saw a solitary house on the mountain ridge – like a temple on the side of the road. The twister bumped against that wall, and stopped moving.

The Elder walked slowly to the wall and kicked at the twister a few times. Then he leaned over, picked up the hat, and tore it apart. He threw the pieces to the ground and stomped on them while shouting,

I told you to run away!

I told you to go with the twister.

I don't want to have to keep waiting for you to leave.

After the Elder tore the hat to pieces, the fresh scent of the straw slowly dissipated. Along that mountain ridge, which had endured scorching weather for so many days, there now appeared a new scent. The Elder rolled what remained of the hat into a ball, then threw it down and stomped on it again, exclaiming, *Aren't you going to run away? This way, you'll never be able to run away. The sun and the drought want to torture me, and even your fucking mother wants to torture me.* As he was saying this, the Elder took a deep breath, then gazed at the hillside beyond Baliban Field. As he was looking, his feet stopped stomping on the remainder of the straw hat, and his mumblings were also cut short like a rope.

Over by the hill, the mountains and plain were covered with fiery red dust, like a translucent wall that swayed back and forth. The Elder stared in disbelief, realizing that what he had seen was actually not a little twister but rather a major wind. As he stood in front of the wall under the searing sun, his heart pounded, as though the wall had collapsed and was crushing him.

He started to rush over to Baliban Hill.

In the distance, the wall of translucent dust began to thicken. It rose and swayed, as though it were the beginning of a flood that was about to bury the entire mountain range.

The Elder reflected, *It's over!* He was afraid this was really the end. *When that twister blew my hat off, it was actually leading me over to the mountain! It wanted to tell me that a strong wind had developed on the hill.* He continued, *I'm afraid*

I let you down, little twister. I really shouldn't have kicked you.
He continued, *There's also my straw hat. It had no qualms
about going wherever the little twister was blowing it, so why
did I have to rip it up? I'm getting old – really old. I may even
be getting a bit senile, and am having trouble distinguishing right
from wrong.* These self-recriminations sprouted from his
mouth like a continuous vine. As he began to calm down,
the wind started to subside, as did the pounding in his
ears – although the sudden silence left him with a piercing
pain in his eardrums. The sunlight also regained its earlier
dynamism, becoming strong and hard. The rays generated
a clear, white squeaking sound in the fields, as though bean
pods were exploding under the searing heat of the sun. The
Elder's pace slowed, and his panting subsided. When he
reached the hill, he stood at the front of his field, and his
breath was cut off by the scene before him.

The seedling had nearly been blown over by the wind,
and was now trembling like a broken finger. Under the hard
sunlight, a dense green sorrow was flowing like a silk thread.

The Elder and the dog decided to relocate to Baliban Hill.

The Elder didn't hesitate and, like an old melon
farmer who has to live in his melon field when the melons
are about to ripen, he relocated to the field. He planted
four posts in the ground next to the seedling, placed a
couple of wooden doors on top of the posts, and draped

four straw mats over them, making a simple shed. Then he hammered some nails to the posts, from which he hung his pot, spoon, and brush. He stuffed his bowls into a flour bag, and hung it under the pot. Finally, he dug a hole for a small oven in the ground under the cliff. Then, he simply waited for the seedling to sprout more leaves.

Given that the Elder had moved to a new location, when night fell he simply couldn't fall asleep. The moon-like white heat was moving through the air. He removed his underwear, which was all that he had been wearing, and sat naked on the bed, smoking. Under the dim light of the pipe, he found himself gazing at that thing between his legs, which was dangling there like a lantern. Finding it extremely ugly, he put his underwear back on and thought, *I am truly old – that is no longer of any use to me, and is no longer capable of bringing me pleasure. It isn't even as valuable to me as the corn seedling. Every single leaf of the seedling gives me enjoyment, like the women standing in the field or chatting next to the well, whom I would admire when I was young.* A languid feeling coursed through his body and he emptied the bowl of his pipe, as the embers fell onto the dark field. Then he woke up the blind dog sleeping next to him.

The Elder asked, *Are you awake?*

Then he added, *You're blind, yet you are sleeping so soundly. Meanwhile, I can see, yet I can't fall asleep.*

The dog crawled over to lick the Elder's hand, and the Elder caressed its head, running his fingers through its fur. As he was smoothing the dog's fur, he noticed that a pair of bright tears had appeared in the animal's empty eye sockets. The Elder wiped away the tears, and said, *This sun, which refuses to die, truly has a black heart. It even burned this dog's eyes.* Upon remembering how the dog's eyes had been seared by the sun, the Elder felt something tugging at his heart. He pulled the dog over and caressed its eyes, as the animal's tears drenched his hand like a pair of mountain springs. *This is something no one could possibly have expected,* the Elder thought. Every time there was a drought, people would always erect an altar at the front of the village and would leave three plates of offerings and two jugs. The jugs would always be full of water, and would have two dragons painted on the side. Then, the villagers would leave a dog tied between the two jugs, and have the dog look up at the sky. When the dog was thirsty they would give it water, and when it was hungry they would give it food, but when it was neither hungry or thirsty they would simply let it bark furiously at the sun. In the past, they would have let this continue for at least three and at most seven days, until the sun eventually retreated in the face of the dog's barks, and there would be wind, rain, or cloudy skies. But this year, they brought in a wild dog from outside the village and tied it in front of the altar, and although the dog barked for half a month, the sun continued to burn bright, rising and setting every day on schedule. Finally, at noon on the sixteenth day, the Elder walked past the altar and noticed that one of the jugs was bone-dry and the bottom of the other was smoldering. The Elder looked at the dog, and saw that its fur was matted together, and when it opened its mouth no sound came out.

The Elder released the dog, and said, *You can leave. It's not going to rain.*

The dog came down from the altar. It took a few steps, then ran into a wall. It turned around, then ran into a tree. The Elder went and grabbed the dog's ear to take a look, and his heart skipped a beat as he realized the dog's eyes had gotten scorched by the sun, and all that was left was a pair of sockets as empty as dry wells.

The Elder had decided to keep the dog.

Now, the Elder thought, *It's fortunate I decided to keep this blind dog, because otherwise I would have been left alone here in the mountains, and who would I have had to talk to?* The weather was getting cooler, as the daytime heat began to subside. The moon and stars overhead began to regain their brightness. There was a sound like water flowing, but the Elder knew that this sound was not from water, nor was it from the trees, the grass, or from insects, but rather from the empty sky itself, which produced a sound of silence out of its extreme stillness. He continued caressing the dog's head, then dragged his hand down its back and patted its rear. Then he returned his hand to the dog's head, by which point the dog was no longer crying. The Elder caressed the animal's fur with one hand, as the dog licked his other hand. That night, the two of them were enveloped by a warm sense of shared fate.

The Elder said, *Blindy, we should live together. Don't you agree? Life is more interesting with a companion.*

The dog licked his palm.

The Elder said, *I don't have much longer to live. If you could keep me company until I die, then I'd be able to die a good death.*

The dog moved from licking the man's fingers to licking his wrist, which seemed to be interminably long.

He said, *Blindy, do you think our corn seedling will bud again?* The dog stopped licking his hand, then nodded. He asked, *Will it bud tonight, or tomorrow? I'm sleepy. Don't nod, because I can't see you anyway. Just answer me – do you think it will bud tomorrow, or tonight?* The Elder leaned against the shed wall and closed his eyes, and the darkness covered his face like a piece of wet gauze. He stopped caressing the dog's back, and his hand came to rest on the dog's head as he fell asleep.

When the Elder woke up, the sun was already three rod-lengths in the sky. He felt a searing pain under his eyelids, so he sat up and rubbed his eyes. When he gazed out at the golden orb that was still hanging there, he cursed, *Fuck your ancestors for eight generations. Watch how one day I'm not going to dig your family's grave.* After this, he noticed that the blind dog was lying next to the corn seedling in the middle of the field. He had a sudden suspicion, and asked, *Has it budded?* The dog nodded, then the Elder climbed out of the shed. When he reached the seedling, he saw that it did indeed have a new bud. The seedling resembled a newly sprouted cassia tree – it was half a finger tall, so tender it seemed as though it would topple over at the slightest touch, and in the sunlight it appeared as glossy as jade.

The Elder wanted to place something over the sprout to shield it from the sun, so he went down to the gully and looked around, but couldn't find anything and eventually returned empty-handed. He stood next to the stove for a while, then grabbed the hoe and walked over to the pagoda tree and broke off a branch, which he brought back and carefully placed over the sprout. Next he climbed onto the shed, retrieved his shirt, and draped it over the branch, so that the sprout could have some shade.

He said, *I can't bear to have another accident.*

He added, *Blindy, you should eat something. What would you like?*

Then he said, *What is there to eat in the morning? Shall we have some corn soup? Then we can cook something tasty for lunch.*

After the sprout grew two new leaves, the Elder returned to the village to look for something to eat. There wasn't a single grain of wheat in his home. He thought that in such a large village, even if each household had only a handful of grain or a pinch of flour, this would be enough for him and the blind dog to survive this devastating drought. However, when he returned to the village, he discovered that the door to each house was locked, and there were cobwebs everywhere. He returned to his own house. He knew perfectly well that the flour jug had already been swept clean, but he still peered inside, then reached in and felt around. After he pulled out his hand, he stuck his fingers in his mouth and sucked on them, and the pure white taste of wheat blossomed in his mouth and surged through his body. He took a deep breath and inhaled the fragrant scent, then went outside and stood in the street. The sun's rays shone down, flowing through the village like a river of gold. In the deathly silence, the Elder heard the sound of sunlight dripping from the roof. He thought indignantly, *Everyone in the entire mountain ridge has fled, and the thieves have either starved to death or died of thirst. Did all of you fucking lock your doors just to stymie me? I'll climb your walls and pry open your doors, and find who has left behind any grain. If you didn't store any grain, then what had you been planning to eat during the drought? And if you didn't leave behind any grain, then why the hell did you bother to lock your doors in the first place?* The Elder stood in the doorway of one family's house. This house belonged to one of his nephews, with whom he shared a surname. The Elder headed to another house, and stopped in the doorway of an old widow's residence. When the widow was younger, she would give the Elder a pair of thick-soled boots every winter. Now she was dead, and her son had inherited this compound. The thought of this house gave the Elder a warm feeling that lingered in his empty heart. The Elder studied the door for a while, then continued on. His footsteps were lonely but resonant, like wood being chopped in the forest. The sound echoed past each family's locked door, flowing by his feet like a dried-up boat. The Elder finally made it through the entire village, by which point the sun had reached its zenith. It was time for lunch, and he mumbled to himself, *If only Blindy were here, then whichever house it told me to break into, I'd immediately scale the wall and go inside.*

The Elder faced the mountain ridge and shouted, *Blindy . . . Blindy! Whose house do you think I should break into?*

The only response the Elder received was deafening silence.

Discouraged, the Elder sat down and smoked his pipe. Then, he returned empty-handed to Baliban Hill. When the Elder approached, the blind dog wagged its tail, then ran up, following his voice, and rubbed its head on his pants. The Elder ignored the dog, and instead went over to the pagoda tree to fetch his hoe. He went to the shed to get a bowl and proceeded to dig a hole. After digging two or three more holes, the Elder finally unearthed a seed he had previously planted. It was golden yellow and completely intact, and was heated by the sun's rays to the point that it burned his hand. The Elder then dug a series of holes at the same intervals at which he had originally planted the seeds, and from each hole he unearthed one or two seeds. By the time he had traversed half the ridge, his bowl was full of seeds.

In this way, he was able to enjoy a dish of fried corn seeds.

As he was eating his fried seeds, the Elder sat with the blind dog under the shadow of the shed and began to chuckle. *Every family has stored some food for me,* he remarked, *so if I go out into the field and dig for a day, I could find enough for the two of us to eat for three more days.* When he did go to another family's fields, however, he found the situation wasn't so simple. He didn't know where exactly the other family had planted their seeds, and didn't know where exactly he should dig. Many families, as they rushed to sow their corn before the rains came, had their children grab hoes and start digging frantically, and the result was that the seeds were planted at different depths and at irregular intervals – not at all like the Elder's perfectly even and regularly spaced holes. In the past, families would never have permitted their children to hoe, but during this drought everything had gotten confused.

As a result, the Elder found that he couldn't dig for one day and obtain sufficient food for him and the dog to survive on for another three days. Instead, he would exert himself all day, and if he was fortunate he'd find enough grain for two days, and if not he'd only end up with enough for one day. His sprout continued to grow, and in the still night it produced a faint and tender sound, like the quiet breathing of a sleeping baby. The Elder and the dog were sitting next to the sprout, resting after having spent all day digging. When they heard the sprout breathing, their joints suddenly felt warm and relaxed. The moon emerged, as round as a woman's face, and hung overhead. The stars sparkled all around it, like buttons on new clothing worn for New Year's, fastened to an unimaginably vast blue silk cloth. At that moment, the Elder suddenly asked the dog, *Blindy, when you were younger, did you do it with a lot of female dogs?*

The dog stared at him blankly.

If you don't want to answer, so be it. The Elder sighed, then lit his pipe. He said to the sky, *It's good to be young. When you're young, you have energy, and at night you can have a woman. If she is very bright, then when you return from the fields, she'll bring you some water; if your face is covered in sweat, she'll hand you a fan; and when it snows, she'll warm up your bedding for you. If you don't sleep soundly with her at night, then when you wake up in the morning she'll urge you to go back to sleep.* The Elder took a long drag on his pipe, then exhaled a cloud of smoke like a long embankment. While patting the dog, he asked, *How is that sort of life any different from that of gods and deities?*

The Elder continued, *Have you lived that sort of life, Blindy?*

The dog was silent.

The Elder said, *Tell me, Blindy, was it not for that sort of life that men came into this world?* The Elder didn't wait for the dog to respond, and instead answered his own question, *I would say yes.* Then he added, *But not when we're old. When we're old, we only live for a tree, a tuft of grass, or a passel of grandchildren. Living, after all, is better than dying.* As the Elder said this, he took another drag on his pipe, and in the dim light he noticed that the sound the corn sprout was making as it grew was reaching out toward his ear like a tender thread. He leaned toward the sprout, and saw that the top, which was already more than knee-high, appeared disheveled. A new leaf was budding from the pale purplish-yellow stem. There were already nine leaves arching out from the corn sprout like bent bows. The Elder stood up, grabbed his hoe, and dug a hole below the sprout. He and the blind dog both urinated into the hole, filling it with three bowls of urine, then refilled it with dirt. Next, he mixed some dirt and water, and made a small pile of mud around the corn sprout. He was afraid that another gust of wind might blow the sprout over, so that night the Elder returned to the village to fetch four reed mats, then erected four poles around the sprout at intervals of four feet, and placed the mats against the poles to form an enclosure. As he was positioning the mats, the Elder said, *Blindy, go to the village and find some rope or string. Any kind will do.* The blind dog zigzagged down the mountain path, and finally, as the moon was setting and the stars were beginning to fade, it returned, holding in its mouth the remains of the Elder's ripped-up straw hat. The Elder used the hat's string to fasten the mats to the poles, and when he ran out of string he used the black thread from his own pants. By the time he had finished, the eastern sky was beginning to brighten.

Between dawn and dusk, that ring of mats surrounded the corn sprout like a small garden in front of the house of a wealthy peasant. The solitary sprout stood there like a flagpole. It was able to enjoy a privileged existence, drinking water and absorbing nutrients, and at midday it was shaded by the reed mats. The sprout grew crazily, and after a week or so it had already reached the top of the enclosure.

The problem was that the sun kept reappearing, and the well would inevitably dry up. The Elder returned to the village every day to fetch some water, and each trip he would have to lower the bucket into the well more than ten times, but even then would end up with half a bucket of sand and murky water. A feeling of terror began to rise out of the well, permeating the Elder's entire being. Finally, one day he lowered the bucket, using the entire length of the rope, but only managed to bring up the equivalent of a small bowl of water. He then had to wait for a long time before another bowlful of water seeped into the bottom of the well.

The well was almost dry, like a tree that had lost all its leaves.

The Elder came up with an idea – before nightfall he lowered his quilt into the well, let it sit there overnight, then the next morning he hauled it up and was able to wring out half a bucketful of water. He then lowered the quilt back into the well, and took the water to the field. He also took the water from washing dishes, from washing his face, and from occasionally washing his clothes – and used it to irrigate the corn sprout. In this way, he managed to make do, and his water supply did not appear excessively limited. As he was again wringing the water from the quilt into the bucket, clouds of steam wafted out. The Elder battled the sun over the right to the steam, exclaiming, *I'm already seventy-two years old. Is there anything I haven't experienced? Do you think I can be defeated by a dried-up well? As long as there is water underground, I'll figure out a way to find it. Sun, if you have the patience, you can try to dry up the water underground.*

In the end, the Elder won the battle.

One day, the Elder dug in his nephew's field continuously from dawn till dusk, but only ended up with half a bowl of corn seeds. The next day he went to another family's field, but didn't manage to find even half a bowl. Over a span of three days, the Elder and the dog had to shift from eating three times a day to eating only twice, and in place of corn soup they instead had to settle for dilute broth. The Elder realized that the situation was becoming quite desperate, but what he couldn't understand was – if each family had sowed their fields with corn seeds that never sprouted – why wasn't the soil full of seeds? Upon seeing the dog's ribs poking out, the Elder broke into a cold sweat. He touched his own cheeks, and found that he could pull his skin several inches from his face, as though his skin was but a piece of cloth draped loosely over his skull. He felt completely drained, and while hauling the quilt up from the bottom of the well he repeatedly had to stop and rest. The Elder thought, *I can't let myself starve to death like this.*

The Elder said, *Blindy, I have no choice but to scale a courtyard wall and break into someone's house.*

He added, *Let's just think of it as borrowing. I'll return everything after there's a harvest.*

The Elder took a sack and staggered back to the village. The dog silently followed him. The Elder curled his toes, so that he was walking on his heels and the tips of his toes, while keeping the arches of his feet elevated so as not to touch the hot ground. The blind dog, meanwhile, would stop every few steps and lick its paws. It seemed as though it took the two of them a year to make it to the village, and when they finally reached a cattle pen near the front of the village, the Elder huddled in the wall's shadow, removed his shoes, and massaged his feet.

The dog also sat in the shade, panting, then peed a drop of urine against the wall.

The Elder said, *Let's borrow some grain from this household*. He removed an axe from his sack and proceeded to smash open the lock on the front entrance. Then he pushed the door open and went inside. He went directly to the doorway leading to the main room, and smashed that lock as well. When he stepped into the main room, he saw that the table was covered with a thick layer of dust, and there were cobwebs everywhere. Between the dust and the cobwebs, there was a memorial tablet, and a portrait of an old man. The figure in the picture was wearing a robe and a mandarin jacket. He had bright eyes that cut through the dust, and his gaze seemed to come to rest on the Elder.

The Elder stared in shock.

This was old Baozhang's house. Old Baozhang had died only three years earlier, and his gaze still appeared sharp and lively. The Elder wondered, *Blindy, are you really blind? How did you know to pee at the entrance of Baozhang's home?* He leaned his axe against the doorway, knelt down and kowtowed three times, then bowed three more times. He said, *Baozhang, the Balou Mountains are several hundred li wide, but now the entire region is in the grip of a once-in-a-millennium drought. All the other residents – including men and women, young and old – have fled, and Blindy and I are the only ones left in the village, or even the entire world. We stayed behind to look after the village, but it has been three days since we had a real meal. Today, we have come to your house to borrow some food, but next year we will definitely return everything. Furthermore, Baozhang, you need not mind us – I already know where each family hid the grain they kept in reserve in case of drought.* Upon saying this, the Elder got up, dusted the dirt from his knees, then carried his grain sack into one of the inner rooms, where he looked in all of the jugs and jars. They were completely empty, but the Elder was not discouraged. It seemed as though he knew that the family's grain wouldn't be stored in such an obvious place. Next, he looked under the bed. Using the light that was coming in through the window, he carefully inspected the area beneath the bed in the eastern room, and thought, *When everyone fled the famine, would they have left their grain in the open for thieves to find? If it were me, I would have hidden mine under my bed.* But, other than a porcelain urine basin, the area under Baozhang's bed was completely empty, without even a speck of dirt. The Elder then moved the empty jugs and jars out of the way, to look under the table and inside the cabinet. The sound of him moving things around echoed through the three-room house. He rummaged about for a long time, until he was covered in dust and cobwebs, but still couldn't manage to find a single grain of wheat.

The Elder dusted off his hands and said, *Baozhang. Ah, Baozhang. When you were still alive, I never did you wrong, and even though I'm six months older than you, I've always called you Elder Brother. If there wasn't any leftover grain in your house, you should have just said so! Instead, you've made me spend half the day looking for nothing, as though I had limitless energy – as though, if I were to leave your house, I wouldn't be able to find any grain elsewhere.*

Baozhang, of course, didn't respond.

When Baozhang didn't respond, the Elder tossed him a glance, and added, *Yes, it's true. You made me kowtow and bow to you for nothing.* Afterward, he patted the head of the blind dog, who was lying in the entranceway, and said, *Let's go. I'm sure we'll have better luck elsewhere.*

The Elder closed the door and hung up the broken lock – leaving the door the way he had found it – then proceeded to enter one house after another. He went to seven houses in a row – and each time he broke the lock on the front door, went inside, and searched their grain jars and jugs, in and around their cabinets, under their beds and tables. He searched each house with a fine comb, but in the end he was unable to find even a single speck of grain. When he emerged from the seventh house, the Elder took a food scale and a horse whip – this family had a horse-drawn carriage, and the Elder had previously helped them drive it – then he went out into the street and stood there at a loss. He dropped the scale and the whip on the side of the road, and asked himself, *Why do I need a scale? If I could find enough grain to weigh on a scale, in the future I could return the correct amount of grain to its owner, but where in the world am I going to find any grain?* He said, *What do I need a whip for? Although I could use a whip like a gun to protect myself* — the Elder had once used a whip to kill a wolf — *the animals in the mountains have all fled and now there isn't even a single rabbit left. Isn't this whip completely useless?* As the sun shone through the cracks in each door, every house was illuminated more brightly than before. The Elder glanced up at the sky, and saw that the sun was already at its zenith. It was lunchtime, but he hadn't smelled the faintest hint of grain. A feeling of desperation surged in his heart. He told the blind dog to sit down in the street, saying, *You should wait here. Since you are completely blind, you wouldn't be able to see where everyone has hidden their grain.* Then he headed over to another alley, where he selected several houses with plenty of sunlight, and broke into them. Yet even after he had entered three more residences, his grain sack remained completely empty. When he reemerged from the alley, the bright sunlight made him appear pale, and a sense of acute sorrow coursed through the deep furrows of his face. The Elder was holding a salt shaker that had half a pinch of salt inside, and he put a single grain of salt into his mouth, then went to put one into the dog's mouth as well.

The dog looked at him inquisitively with its blind eyes, seeming to ask, *Could it be that you didn't find any food?*

The Elder didn't answer. Instead, he picked up the whip, stood in the middle of the road, and began whipping the sun. The thin leather whip writhed through the air like a snake, producing a series of sharp, explosive cracks. The Elder whipped the sun until its fragments fell to the earth like pear petals, covering the ground with shattered sunlight, and the entire village seemed to be filled with the sound of New Year's fireworks. Only after the Elder was exhausted and covered in sweat, did he finally put away the whip.

Deeply disappointed, the blind dog stood in front of the Elder, as its eye sockets grew moist.

The Elder said, *Blindy, don't be afraid. In the future, whenever I have a bowl of grain, I'll give you half. I would rather starve than let you die of hunger.*

The blind dog's eyes filled with tears. The teardrops fell to the ground, creating two bean-like depressions in the earth.

Let's go. The Elder picked up the salt shaker, as well as the whip and the scale. He said, *Let's return to the hill and dig for more seeds.*

After they had only walked a couple of steps, the Elder came to an abrupt halt. He saw a swarm of rats, each of which was round and fat, as though it were a year with a bumper harvest. The rats waited under the shade of the wall, staring uneasily at the village, the Elder, and the blind dog. Suddenly, it was as if a door in the Elder's mind had swung open.

The Elder laughed.

This was the first time the Elder had laughed since the other villagers fled, and his crackling laugh was hoarse and brittle, like slow-roasted soybeans. The Elder said, *You can starve the sky and you can starve the earth, but you certainly can't starve this old man.*

The Elder led the blind dog over to the terrified rats, and said, *Blindy, do you know where all the grain is hidden? I do. I know.*

That night, the Elder dug up three rat nests and collected a *sheng* of corn seeds. The Elder spent the first half of the night sleeping lightly in the shed, then around midnight – under the stars and the bright moon, and as the ground was covered with a bright sheet of moonlight – the Elder told the dog to stand guard by the corn sprout while he went to the center of the field, where he sat down and held his breath. He stayed this way for a while, until he was able to hear rats rustling around. This was not the sound of rats playing happily, but rather they were fighting over food. The Elder pressed his ear to the ground, confirming where exactly the sounds were coming from, then used a stake to mark the spot. Next, he went back to fetch his hoe and began digging. Sure enough, three feet from the stake and one foot down, he found a rat's nest in which there was the equivalent of half a bowl of corn seeds. The Elder didn't leave a single seed behind, even scooping up the rat droppings along with the grain. Then he went to a second spot, and followed the same process.

The Elder's days were busy. In the morning he would wake and go to the village to haul the water-soaked quilt up from the well. After returning to his field and eating breakfast, he would pick out the rat droppings from the grain, and then put the grain in a bowl. After the bowl was full, he would bury it next to the corn sprout. After lunch, he would need to take a nap, and although the sun shone brightly into the shed, it wasn't as sweltering as it was outside, and sometimes a cool breeze would even blow through. He would sleep soundly, and when he woke up the sun would already be over the western mountains. He would then go back to the village to wring another half a bucket of water from the quilt, after which dusk would arrive as usual. He would have dinner and then would sit with the dog by the corn sprout in the cold fear and solitude of the night. He would ask the dog and the sprout some questions that had been troubling him, such as, *Why do crops grow one leaf at a time?* Neither the dog nor the sprout was able to offer an answer, so the Elder simply lit his pipe, took a long drag, and said, *Let me tell you. It's because they are crops, which is why they have to grow one leaf at a time. And because others are plants, they grow two leaves at a time.* Some nights, the wind would blow as usual, and the Elder would ask the dog and the sprout even more profound questions, such as, *You knew? When old Baozhang was still alive, a scholar once came to the village and said that this earth was spinning around, and each time it spun around once, this was a day. You tell me, wasn't this scholar simply farting in the wind? If the earth were spinning, then why aren't we knocked out of our beds when we sleep in the village at night? Why does water not spill out of the water jugs, or stream out of wells? Why do people always walk with their heads pointed toward the sky?* The Elder added, *Based on what that man said, the earth must be sucking us in, so that we don't fall out of our beds at night. But just think, if the earth were sucking us in, then how would we be able to lift our feet when we walk?* As the Elder was discussing these sorts of questions, which were as deep and murky as a dark hole, he would stop smoking his pipe and assume a very solemn expression. Finally, he laid out all of his questions in front of the dog and the sprout, then fell to the ground, such that his face was now parallel with the sky. He let the moonlight wash over him, and said, *I was too polite to that scholar, and was too concerned with trying not to make him lose face. He stayed in the village for three days, but I didn't ask him about any of this. I was afraid that if he were unable to answer my questions, he might lose face in front of the entire village.* The Elder added, *To eat and survive, that scholar relied on his learning, which I couldn't bring myself to shatter.*

The cornstalk continued growing smoothly. Its leaves were now as wide as a man's palm, extending layer after layer from the ground up to the reed mats, and beyond. By now the stalk was already twice as high as the mats, and the sound of it growing at night had become a dull roar. In a few more days, the stalk would reach its full height. In order to make it easier to enter the enclosure, the Elder cut open one of the mats. Seven days earlier he had gone in to compare his height with that of the stalk, and found that the stalk already reached his neck, and two days later it was up to his forehead. Within half a month, the stalk should start producing ears, and after three months the corn should be ripe. The Elder thought about how, in this barren and desolate mountain range, he would have succeeded in growing an ear of corn, and how he would collect a bowlful of corn, with each grain being as precious as a pearl. Eventually, the rains would finally come, the villagers would return to the village, and they would be able to use this bowl of corn seeds for sowing. In this way, the mountain range could once again be covered in endless fields of green corn. The Elder thought, *After I die, they should erect a plaque reading* BOUNDLESS BENEFICENCE *in front of my grave.*

The Elder continued talking to himself, saying, *I am indeed full of beneficence,* and as he was saying this, he slipped into a dream. Later, still asleep, he climbed down from his shed, went over to the cornstalk, and hoed around it. In the quiet night, the rhythmic and resonant sound of his hoeing was like a melodic line in a folk music performance. Throughout the mountain range, the sound spread far and wide. After he finished hoeing, the Elder didn't return to bed, and instead he took his hoe to another location, where he again held his breath to listen for signs of a rat's nest filled with corn seeds. When he woke up the next morning, he discovered that his bowl, which had been empty, was now full of corn and rat droppings. He stood next to the bowl for a long time, staring in shock.

There was a grain sack hanging from one of the shed posts, and it was already half full of corn. Three days earlier, at around noon, the Elder had been sleeping and the blind dog had run over and tugged at him until he woke up. The dog then dragged him out to the corner of a field located several dozen steps away. When they arrived, the Elder discovered a rat's nest full of corn. When the Elder took the corn back and weighed it, he found that it was about four or five *qian*. So, it turned out that the blind dog could find rat nests as well. The dog would run around a field, sniffing the ground, and whenever it found a nest, it would start barking.

As his grain sack grew fat, the Elder stopped going out to the fields in the middle of the night to find rat nests. Instead, he would take the dog, whereupon each of the nests would be revealed – though half of them actually contained no grain. The Elder and the blind dog now had a surplus of grain, and within a few days, the grain sack was filled to the brim. However, just when the Elder felt that he could sleep comfortably and was able to forget about having to frantically dig up all of the rat nests on the ridge, it turned out that the rats had stopped digging up the corn seeds and taking them back to their nests for storage, and instead had begun competing with the Elder to see who could consume their stored grain the fastest. One day – when the sun appeared much nearer than it had in the past and the soil along the mountain ridge had become like a burning-red iron plate – the Elder couldn't sleep, and decided to weigh his grain. He took his scale, and when he weighed the grain in the shade, it came out to one *liang,* but when he took it into the sunlight, the scale instead read 1.2 *liang*. The Elder was startled. He took the scale up to the hill, where the sun was shining even brighter, and there the scale read 1.25 *liang*.

Astonished, the Elder found that when the sun was shining brightly, its weight could register on the scale. The Elder ran up to the mountain ridge, and found that at the top of the ridge the scale read 1.31 *liang*. After subtracting the one-*liang* weight of the plate itself, that meant the sunlight weighed 0.31 *liang,* which is to say 3.1 *qian*. The Elder quickly climbed four more mountain ridges, each taller than the last, and found that at the top of the tallest ridge the sunlight weighed 5.3 *qian*.

From this point on, the Elder repeatedly weighed the sunlight. When the sun first came out in the morning, the sunlight around the shed weighed two *qian,* by midday it had increased to four *qian,* and at sunset it had reverted back to two *qian*.

The Elder also weighed his rice bowl and water bucket. Once, as he was weighing the blind dog's ear, the dog knocked the scale's balance arm and struck his face, so he hit the dog in the head.

By the time the Elder decided to weigh the corn seeds again, he had already been weighing the sunlight for four days, and had eaten several servings of corn. When he added up the weight of all the corn, the Elder stared in shock. It turned out that the remainder would only last him and the blind dog for another half a month, at most. It was then that it occurred to him that it had been several days since he and the blind dog had gone out to the fields to look for rat nests.

It was already too late! In just a few days, the rats, as though they had received advance notice, had consumed all of the grain they had stored up in their nests. The Elder spent an entire afternoon leading the blind dog to seven different hillside fields, where the two of them dug up thirty-one rat nests. They worked until they were about to drop, but only managed to dig up eight *liang* of corn. At sunset, the sun's blood-colored light shone down from the western mountains onto the ridge, the corn leaves that had been curled up during the day finally began to uncurl and exhale. The Elder brought over that half-bowl of corn mixed with rat droppings, and it suddenly occurred to him that the rats up on the ridge were now competing with him and the blind dog for grain.

The Elder wondered, *Where have they taken all of their grain?*

He thought, *No matter how clever they may be, they'll never be able to outsmart me.*

That night, the Elder and the blind dog went to listen for rats in an even more distant field. They visited three different fields that night, but didn't hear a sound. Just as the eastern sky was beginning to lighten, the Elder returned with the dog, and he asked, *Have the rats moved away? If so, where did they go? Wherever they went, there must be grain, so we have to find them.* The sunlight shone down on the dog's empty eye sockets. The dog cocked its head and walked away with its back to the sun without hearing what the Elder was saying.

The Elder asked, *Could the rats be hiding somewhere, to compete with us?*

The dog paused, then turned and followed the sound of the Elder's footsteps.

When they arrived at the shed, the Elder went to inspect the cornstalk, and found that the stem was now as wide as a child's wrist. Then he prepared to return to the village to fetch some water. He collected two empty buckets, and wanted to take the dog along with him. The dog, however, was lying motionless under the shed. The Elder said, *Let's go. Let's go to the village and see which houses have rats in them, so that we can know where to look for grain.* Only then did the dog get up and accompany him. In the village, apart from two rats that had drowned in the well, they didn't see a single rodent in the streets, alleyways, or the entranceways of the houses whose doors they had pried open. When the Elder returned to Baliban Hill with his load of water, he discovered that everything was in disarray. When they were half a *li* from the hillside field, the dog began to act ill at ease, and periodically barked a purplish yelp. The Elder quickened his pace. He climbed the ridge, and when the field appeared before him, the dog suddenly stopped barking and instead began running like crazy toward their shed. In the process it almost fell off the cliff. The hard sunlight on the ground was shattered by the dog's footsteps, producing an explosive sound like a bottle shattering, and its sharp, frantic barks saturated the fields like red blood.

The Elder stared in shock.

The Elder was standing at the far end of the field, and in the intervals between the dog's barks, he could hear the squeaking of rats, like drizzling rain. Then, he went to the shed in the middle of the field and saw that the grain sack he had hung on one of the poles had fallen. Its contents had spilled onto the hardened ground. A black mass of rats – numbering three to five hundred, or perhaps even a thousand or more – were fighting over the spilled corn seeds. They were running back and forth, and the seeds rolled around under their feet and dribbled out of their mouths. The sound of them chewing mingled with their excited laughter, and the sound rained down on the hillside like a thunderstorm. The Elder stood there speechless, as the dog ran over and bumped its head on one of the poles. Blood spurted into the air, whereupon the dog and the rats fell into a stupor. After a moment they came to their senses, and the dog once again began running around barking, becoming so frantic that it hit one of the posts with its paw. The rats didn't realize the dog was blind, and were so terrified by its frenzy that they began crying darkly. The result was a cacophony of cursing and terror, as the mountain ridge, which had been deathly quiet for the past two months, suddenly began to boil over. As the Elder ran through the mass of rats, he stepped on one and heard a scream, as hot blood splattered over his other foot. The Elder ran to the enclosure and dove inside, and as he feared, there were two thirsty rats eating that watery-green cornstalk. When the rats heard the Elder barge in, they paused and then ran out through an opening in the side of the enclosure. Upon seeing that the cornstalk was standing there intact, the Elder relaxed. He turned and left the enclosure, and saw that several starving rats were still scurrying around in the grain sack under the shed. He grabbed the hoe leaning against the mats and used it to hit the sack, whereupon a multitude of red droplets spurted out. He struck the sack several times in a row, as rat fur flew everywhere and the ground became splattered with blood. The remaining several dozen rats shrieked in terror and shot out in all directions, disappearing in the blink of an eye.

The blind dog stopped barking.

The Elder leaned against his hoe, breathing heavily.

The Balou Mountains suddenly became very silent – a thick and heavy silence that was several times more ponderous than it had been in the past. The Elder guessed that hundreds and thousands of rats must be hiding nearby, and would come rushing back as soon as he left. He glanced at the mountains around him, then sat down on the hoe handle and picked up the corn seeds that had spilled. He said, *Blindy, what are we going to do? Can you guard this?* The blind dog lay on the ground that had been warmed by the sunlight and stuck out its tongue. The Elder said, *I don't have any water. I, you, and the cornstalk – none of us has a single drop to drink.*

The Elder didn't cook any food that day. He and the blind dog went hungry, and after nightfall they stood guard by the enclosure around the cornstalk. They were afraid it would take a couple of rats just a few bites to gnaw through the stalk, so they kept watch until dawn. In the end, they didn't see any rats. Around noon the following day, the Elder noticed that one of the leaves had begun to curl in the sunlight, and only then did he go fetch a pair of empty buckets.

The Elder said, *Blindy, I want you to stand guard by the cornstalk.*

The Elder said, *You can lie in the shade, and keep your ear to the ground. If you hear even the faintest sound, then bark loudly in that direction.*

The Elder said, *I'm going to go fetch some water, and you must stay alert.*

When the Elder returned with half a bucket of water, everything appeared to be all right. The only problem was that when he had hauled the quilt out of the well, he found that it contained four drowned rats whose soaked fur was full of fleas. The Elder ate his meal, then placed the corn seeds on a couple of stones. As he was grinding the seeds, he began to feel anxious. His corn reserve had been devoured by the rats to the point that he now had only half a sack left. The Elder weighed the remainder, and found that he still had six *jin* and two *liang*. If he consumed only half a portion for each meal, three times a day, then he and the dog would consume one *jin* each day. What would they do in six days, after their provisions were exhausted?

The sun was about to set, and the mountain ridge to the west was drenched in a bloody red aura. The Elder gazed at the myriad colors under this sheet of red, and it occurred to him that he would soon use up their food, and would run out of water two or three days later. He looked at the cornstalk, and saw that the top had begun to turn pink. He tried to calculate how long it would be until it started producing tassel, and how long until it produced an ear. It occurred to him that many, many days had already passed, and he could no longer remember what day or even what month it was. He noticed that apart from not knowing whether it was day or night, morning or dusk, sunrise or moonset – these sorts of time periods that occur each day – he had even lost all awareness of time. His mind was a complete blank. He said, *Blindy, have we already passed the first day of autumn?* But he didn't look at the dog, and instead merely mumbled to himself, *For all we know, we've already entered the following solar term, and it's generally around this time that corn begins producing tassel.*

The Elder squinted, and proceeded to grind the corn seeds on the stone's surface. He watched as the blind dog sniffed the ground, then picked up a dead rat and carried it over to the gully. When the dog was several feet from the edge of the gully, it shook its head and tossed the rat in.

The Elder noticed a faint stench.

The dog returned and grabbed another dead rat, then took it to the edge of the gully as well.

The Elder needed a calendar. He stared at the dog, and it occurred to him that without a calendar, there were no dates; and with no dates, he had no way of knowing when the corn would ripen. There were perhaps still thirty or forty days until the autumn harvest. But what would he eat during this intervening period? The rats had consumed all of the seeds in the fields. The Elder raised his head and heard shrill screams coming from the west. He peered into the distance, and between the two mountain peaks he could see the sun being swallowed by another mountain peak. The remaining blood-red stain flowed from the peaks down to the foot of the mountains, then back up to the Elder. The entire world became completely silent. It was once again the quietest time of day, between dusk and nightfall. In the past, this would be when chickens returned to roost and sparrows went back to their nests, and the entire world would be filled with rain-like chirping. But now there wasn't a sound. There were no livestock, no sparrows, and even the crows had fled the drought. There was only silence. The Elder saw that the setting sun's bloodlike glow was becoming fainter and fainter, and he listened as it was blown farther away from him, like a sheet of silk. He collected the ground-up seeds from the stone and thought, *Another day has ended, but how will I endure tomorrow, when the sun is again overhead?*

Three more days elapsed, and no matter how hard he tried to economize, he still used up more than half of the remaining corn. The Elder wondered, *Where have all the rats gone? What are they living on?*

On the fourth night, he summoned the blind dog over to the cornstalk, and said, *I want you to keep watch, and if you hear any movement, just bark.* Then, the Elder grabbed a hoe and headed north up the mountain ridge. When he reached a field located farthest from the village, he placed his hoe in the middle of the field, then sat down on the handle. He sat there until the dawn light was visible in the east, but didn't hear a sound. The next day he led the blind dog out to this field, and the dog helped him find seven rat nests. After he dug up the nests, however, he discovered that inside there were no rats or grain, and apart from some droppings the only thing he found was hot, rocky soil. He searched for the hoe marks from when the field's owner originally sowed the corn, then dug several new holes – but still didn't find any seeds.

It finally struck him that in this entire mountain ridge there wasn't a single speck of food left.

Blindy, the Elder said, *what do you think? Are we going to starve to death?*

The blind dog stared into the sky with its eyes that were as dark as the bottom of a well.

The Elder said, *I don't think the stalk will ever mature.*

They entered the fifth night, and as soon as the sun set, darkness arrived with a crackling sound. The entire mountainside was covered in moonless and starless darkness. At this point, the desiccated old trees on the mountainside had just received some moisture, and they quickly let out a delicate sigh. The Elder sat down with his dog next to the cornstalk, and scratched his nose with one of the leaves. He inhaled several gulps of fragrant air, whereupon the scent of grain rushed toward his intestines like a horse-drawn carriage careening down the street. He waited until the odor reached his belly, then he clinched his abdomen, trapping the odor inside his stomach. As he was doing this, he heard the faint sound of moonlight falling to earth, and said, *Blindy, you should come over and have a few bites. That way you won't be hungry.* He called to the animal a couple of times, but didn't see any movement. When he turned, he saw that the dog was lying on a mat like a pile of mud. He reached over to touch it, then jumped back in alarm. The dog's stomach was poking through its skin, so sharp that it cut his hand like a knife. The Elder then felt his own stomach. He first peeled off a layer of cracked, dirty skin and tossed it to the ground, then he touched the soft skin beneath it, and found that he could feel his lower vertebrae poking through from his back.

Blindy, the Elder said, *look, the moon has emerged. You should sleep, because if you do you won't be hungry. You can treat your dreams as though they were food.*

The dog stood up and staggered to the shed.

Don't climb onto the shed, the Elder said. *Just sleep on the ground. That way you can save your energy.*

The dog returned to where it had originally been lying, and stopped moving.

The crescent moon slowly emerged from behind a cloud, and the mountain ridge appeared as though it were covered in water. In the haze, the Elder stared into the dark night, and prayed, *Am I about to starve to death? Please give me some grain, so that I may survive a few more days. At the very least, I want to outlive the dog, so that after it dies I can pick a good spot and bury it. That way the rats won't be able to devour its corpse, and won't be able to prevent it from returning to the mortal world in the next life. After the dog dies, please let me survive to watch this cornstalk. After the corn is ripe, don't let me die. I must make it until the next rainfall – until the villagers return to the ridge, so that I can give them this ear of corn. This corn belongs to the mountain ridge.* As the Elder was praying, he caressed a corn leaf with one hand, while continuing to peel off some dead skin from his stomach. As the Elder was about to go to sleep, he gently placed his feet on the dog's back, and said, *Go to sleep, Blindy. After you fall asleep, you'll forget your hunger.* With this, the Elder's eyelids slammed shut and he staggered off into dreamland.

As the Elder was sleeping, he kicked his feet that had been resting on the dog's back, and the dog's barking shattered his sleep like a stone. The Elder sat up and heard the faint sound of rats squeaking on the ridge, and the sound of their tiny paws. The dog was standing outside of the reed mats, barking in the direction of the mountain ridge. The Elder patted the dog's head and told it to go back inside the enclosure to guard the cornstalk. This happened just as the sun was about to rise, the moonlight was beginning to fade, and the air had a faint scent of moisture. The Elder climbed onto the shed and squatted down on the side facing the mountain ridge. He noticed there was a strong, dark-red rat stench, and there was also dust flying everywhere. He blinked his eyes, but all he could see was a cloud-like mass over the mountain road, rapidly moving south. He climbed back down off the shed, afraid that the swarm of rats would suddenly turn around and begin rushing toward the stalk. He looked at the enclosure, and saw that the stalk was still standing straight. The blind dog's ears perked up, and the Elder patted its head and said, *You mustn't bark. You mustn't remind the rats we are here. They know that wherever there are people, there will also be food.*

At that point, the roar on the mountain ridge, which sounded like an approaching thunderstorm, suddenly died down. The Elder patted the dog's head again, then quietly made his way toward the ridge. When he arrived, he saw that a steady stream of rats, in groups of ten or twenty, were breaking rank and, squeaking loudly, were heading south. He couldn't believe his eyes – the road, which had previously been as hard as an iron plate, was now covered in a finger-thick layer of dust. The rats' paw prints piled on top of one another, to the point that there wasn't enough empty space between them to insert a needle.

The Elder stood by the road, staring in shock.

The Elder thought, *Where could they all be going?*

Perhaps this drought will continue indefinitely. The Elder thought, *If the drought wasn't going to last, why would the rats flee? Isn't it true that the rats will always have vegetation to eat, and the only thing they fear is lack of water? Given that the rats are fleeing, it's obvious that the drought is going to persist for a lot longer.* But when the Elder turned to leave, he once again heard the sound of rain coming from the north. He knew, however, that this was not in fact rain, but rather another swarm of rats. He shuddered, then stood on an elevated point and gazed out into the distance. As he did, the blood suddenly froze in his veins. He saw that what was streaming down the mountain appeared to be a wall of water surging along the road, but in fact it was a flood-like mass of shrieking rats. The wave of rats rose and fell, and as they approached, their sound changed from that of a drizzle to a torrential downpour. Countless rats leaped up like fish jumping out of water, then fell back into the sea of rodents. The sky was already beginning to brighten, and the air was filled with a foul stench. The Elder's palms became covered in sweat, and he knew that if this wave of rats were to turn around, then he, the blind dog and the cornstalk would be doomed. The rats were crazed with hunger, and were capable of chewing a man's face off. The Elder wanted to run back and tell the blind dog that it mustn't move a muscle, but it was already too late. Like a dark cloud, the wave of rats surged forward. The Elder hid under the branches of a pagoda tree, though the tree was only as thick as his arm. Several rats at the front were enormous – as large as weasels or small cats – and were covered in shimmering gray fur. The Elder had never seen such large rats, and it occurred to him that these must be what people used to call rat kings. He saw that those rats had bright green eyes that sparkled with a bright blue light. They leaped forward like horses, and with each leap they could travel at least a foot and a half. The dust they kicked up covered their backs like gray felt. The Elder squeezed his throat to stifle a sneeze. The sky was growing light, and the cool dawn was approaching as usual. Snow-white clouds were drifting across the bright blue sky, but the sun was brighter than ever. If it weren't, would these rats be fleeing like this? The Elder slipped out from behind the tree, but not a single rat was willing to look straight at him. They seemed to view him as no longer human, but rather an extension of the sky, the sun or the searing drought. The Elder stood there motionless watching the rats rush past, and could hear them falling off the road, like ripe persimmons. What he couldn't understand was how were the rats able to come together to form such an enormous pile? They seemed to be under orders to march south, but what was in the south? Was there grain and water and shade? To the east there was the golden sun, and the Elder suddenly noticed that the rats' eyes had all turned bright red, and appeared to roll down the street like a wave of pearls. Hundreds and thousands of rats that had been pushed off the road began running through the fields on either side, only to disappear in the blink of an eye.

The sun came out, and strand after strand of fur fluttered in the sunlight, like willow catkins and poplar blossoms. The Elder stood on the ridge and sighed, then proceeded back down. His footsteps echoed softly in the morning air, sounding old and listless. When he reached the cornstalk, he saw that the blind dog was staring at the mountain ridge with its blind eyes, as sweat dripped from the tips of its ears.

The Elder asked, *What are you afraid of?*

The dog didn't respond, and instead it simply lay down beside him.

The Elder asked, *Are you afraid there will be a catastrophe?*

The dog still didn't answer, and instead it simply looked at the cornstalk.

The Elder stared in surprise, noticing that on the stalk's leaves there were countless white dots, like sesame seeds. These were the sorts of dry patches that usually only appear during periods of prolonged drought. However, despite the current drought, this stalk had never lacked water. The Elder had dug an irrigation moat around the stalk, to which he had added water virtually every day. He squatted down and lifted the dirt in the moat, and found that under a finger-thick layer of dry soil there was another layer of dirt so wet you could virtually pick up water droplets with your fingers. The Elder grabbed a fistful of this wet soil and realized that those dry patches were a result not of the drought, but rather of the rat stench that pervaded the entire mountainside.

Of all manure, rat excrement is the strongest and the most pungent, the Elder thought. *Given that this stench has sur-rounded the stalk all night, how could the stalk have possibly avoided developing dry patches?* He pressed his ear to the leaves, and found he could hear the squeaking sound made by the dry patches as they expanded. When he turned to smell the air, he noticed a wave of dark, dry rat stench wafting over – flowing toward the cornstalk like a river.

That is to say, the stalk was about to die.

If the stalk hoped to survive, there would need to be a sudden downpour that would wash away this poison-ous stench covering the entire mountainside, and wash away the poisonous air from the stalk itself.

The blind dog sensed the Elder's alarm. The Elder said, *Blindy, you should stand guard while I return to the village to fetch some water.* Not waiting to see if the dog was going to respond, the Elder picked up the empty buckets and headed into the village.

By this point, the village was completely silent. There was a layer of rat excrement by the side of the road, and an unrelenting sun shone through the cracks in the front door of each house. The Elder headed straight for the well. As he was hauling up the quilt from the bottom of the well, he noticed that the rope was so light it seemed as though there was nothing there; and whereas in the past he would hear the sound of water dripping down, now there was nothing. The Elder peered inside, and turned white as a sheet.

After a long pause, the Elder finally hauled up the remainder of the rope. The quilt was no longer tied to the other end, and instead all that remained was a layer of damaged cloth covered with bloated rat carcasses.

The quilt had been devoured by starving rats that had fallen into the well.

The Elder went into someone's house to look for another quilt or some sheets.

The Elder first went to the houses where he had previously searched for grain, but each time he arrived at a house he would merely pause in the doorway. The entire village had been swept clean by the rats. In every

house, the chests, tables, cabinets, beds, and so forth –
everything that had previously contained clothing or food
– had been chewed up like a bowl of sunflower seeds.
A delicate mix of wood odor and rat stench filled each
room and drifted into the courtyard.

The Elder entered more than ten houses, but emerged
from each empty-handed.

When he walked out through the village alleyway,
the Elder was carrying three bamboo poles. He tied the
poles together, then went to an outhouse in the rear
courtyard of another house and fetched a wooden bowl
used to scoop excrement – every family's stove bellows,
chopping boards, wooden bowls and pottery bowls had
been completely gnawed by the rats – and he tied it to
the end of the bamboo poles. He then dipped the bowl
three times into the well to get water, but all he brought
up were more rats. Using the sunlight shining overhead,
the Elder peered into the well, and he saw that there was
in fact no water at the bottom. Instead, the bottom of
the well was covered in a pile of rats, like a storage cel-
lar full of rotten sweet potatoes. There were also some
live rats running over the bodies of the dead ones. The
live rats would climb a few feet up the sides of the well
then fall down again, as their anguished squeals rose
through the shaft.

The Elder carried the empty buckets back to Baliban Hill.

The mountain range stretched endlessly in all directions. Dozens of *li* away, where the mountains touched the horizon, it appeared as though there were fires burning brightly. When the Elder reached the hill, the blind dog ran over. The Elder reported that the well was completely dry, and full of rats. He asked the dog whether there were any rats here, but the dog shook its head. The Elder said, *You and I will be killed by the rats, as will the cornstalk. We won't survive more than a few days.*

Disappointed, the dog stood in the shade of the shed, staring at the sky.

After putting down his bucket, the Elder went inside the enclosure to take a look, and found that each of the dry spots on the leaves was now as large as a fingernail. For what seemed like an eternity, the Elder stood silently in front of the stalk, staring as dry spots on the eleventh leaf expanded and merged together until the leaf came to resemble a dried-out bean pod. He blinked his sleepy eyes, and blue veins protruded from his neck like old roots sticking out of the ground. He left the enclosure, grabbed a whip from the shed, and aimed it at the center of the sun, then whipped the sun more than a dozen times – producing a multitude of shimmering shadows. Eventually, the veins in his neck receded, and he hung the whip back where he had found it, fetched the buckets, and proceeded silently up the ridge.

The dog faced the Elder, its melancholy black eyes full of tears. When the Elder's footsteps faded away, the dog finally turned away, lying down in the sunlight under the cornstalk.

The Elder had gone to fetch water.

The Elder realized that the swarm of rats must be coming from a place where there was water, otherwise how could the rats have survived the drought for so long? The Elder thought, *It must be a lack of food that is driving them to flee, because if there had been food, why would they have devoured all of the woodwork in the village?* The Elder thought, *This mass exodus must not be due to a lack of water.* The sun's rays were bright red, and as the Elder walked alone through the mountain ridge, he could count every ray as it streaked past. The pair of buckets dangling from his shoulder pole knocked plaintively against each other, as the soil under his feet seemed to be sighing. The Elder heard this knocking and sighing, and felt a sense of desolation that seemed vaster than all of the world's drought-plagued land. He visited three villages in a row, and found that in each of them the dried-up wells were full of grass and straw, without even a hint of mold or rot. The Elder decided not to go into the villages to seek water – because if there had been water, then why would the villagers have fled in the first place? Instead, he proceeded from one gully to another, searching for any trace of moisture. Finally, he was walking through a narrow ridge when he noticed some thatch grass growing in the shade of the stone. He exclaimed, *Fuck, how could there not be a way forward?* Then he sat down on the stone to rest, and proceeded to pull up some grass, blade by blade. He sucked out the juice and swallowed the chewed-up remains. He said to himself, *If this ravine doesn't have any water either, I'm definitely going to bash my head in.*

He proceeded toward the ravine, breathing heavily, as though winter had suddenly fallen in front of him. He wasn't sure how far he had walked. When he was chewing the grass, the reddish-white sun was still hanging over the mountain ridge to the west, but now he noticed that the cracked earth under his feet had been replaced by white sand and the sun appeared blood red.

By the time the Elder found a tiny spring, it was already dusk. He first noticed that the white sand under his feet had turned light red from the humidity, and his feet, which were burning hot from walking all day, suddenly enjoyed a trace of coolness. Walking on the wet sand, the Elder proceeded into the ravine, and when it became so narrow that it felt as though it were pressed against his shoulders, the sound of dripping water streamed over him, like music. The Elder looked up, and saw a sheet of green heading toward him. The Elder stopped. He had not seen this much grass in more than five months, and had almost forgotten what it looked like. There was sedge grass and thatch grass, and also small white, red and reddish-white flowers. Under the searing sun, a strong scent of fresh vegetation rolled noisily through the ravine. The Elder's throat began to tighten, and an irresistible thirst arrived at his cracked lips. He saw that a few steps in front of him, under the cliff, there was a spring and a small pool. The pool was partially covering that small plot of grass, as if the grass were growing out from under a mirror.

Just as the Elder was about to drop his buckets and run over to drink from the pool, he paused. He repeatedly swallowed a mouthful of phlegm as he stood there without moving. He saw that behind the mound of grass there was a wolf – a yellow wolf as large as the blind dog. The wolf had bright green eyes and initially seemed surprised by the Elder's appearance, but when it realized he was carrying a pair of buckets, its gaze became fierce and its forelegs stiffened as though it were ready to pounce.

The Elder stood there motionless, staring intently. He knew that this pool was the reason the wolf had not run away. The Elder discreetly looked down, and saw that on the ground next to the bucket there was a mess of fur and feathers. Suddenly realizing that the wolf must have been hiding by the pool waiting for other creatures to come drink, the Elder shuddered with terror. Seeing how emaciated the wolf was, he figured it must have been waiting there for several days. The Elder saw that there was a blood stain on the sand a couple of paces away, as well as quite a few rat heads and other remains. It was only then that he noticed the sharp, fresh stench of rotting meat. The Elder's palms became sweaty and his legs grew weak, as the wolf took a step toward him. At that instant, however, the Elder leaned over, placed the buckets on the ground, and swung his shoulder pole through the air, aiming for the wolf's head.

The wolf took a step back, as the fury in its eyes seemed to overflow and tumble to the ground.

The Elder continued to stare at the wolf.

The wolf also stared at the Elder.

Their gazes collided. In the desolate gorge, the crackling sound of their bright gazes echoed back and forth, and the sound of dripping water resonated explosively around them. The sun was about to set behind the mountains, and time rushed past their interlocked gazes like a herd of horses. The blood-red glow on the cliff in front of them began to fade, as cool air began to descend down the mountain. At some point, the Elder's forehead became covered in sweat, and a feeling of exhaustion rose up from his feet, gradually expanding as it progressed upward from his calves to his thighs. He knew he could not continue like this. He had been walking all day, while the wolf had simply been lying here waiting. He hadn't had anything to drink all day, but the wolf could drink from the spring at any time. He furtively licked his dry lips, which felt as jagged as a bed of thorns. He thought, *Can this wolf possibly drink all of this water?* Then he said out loud, *Hey, if you let me have some water, I'll make you a bowl of corn paste soup.* As the Elder was saying this, he gripped his pole tighter and tighter. The pole was aimed at the wolf's head, and even the hooks tied to each end of the carrying pole remained frozen in place.

The wolf's eyes gradually dimmed. The wolf closed its eyes, but immediately opened them again. The Elder saw that there was a hint of moisture in its hard gaze.

The Elder heard the sound of the setting sun drift over the mountains like a falling leaf. The Elder put down the pole he was holding, placing it on a clump of grass.

The Elder said, *Tomorrow I will bring you a bowl of food.*

The wolf pulled back its front paws, then turned and slowly circled around the edge of the pond, heading toward the opening of the gully. After taking several steps, the wolf stopped and looked back. The Elder watched until the wolf was several dozen paces away, before he finally released his grip and let the pole fall to the ground. He collapsed to a squatting position and shivered violently as he wiped the sweat from his forehead, and it was only then that he realized that even his underwear, which was the only thing he was wearing, was soaked in sweat.

After a long sigh, the Elder found that he lacked the strength to stand. He continued squatting there until finally he scooted forward to the side of the pool, where he lay down and drank from it like an ox. In the blink of an eye, the cool water entered through his mouth and permeated down to the soles of his feet. He drank until his belly was full, then washed his face. Seeing that the red sunlight at the top of the cliff was as thin as a sheet of paper, he picked up the bucket of water and placed it next to the pool, then removed his underwear.

The Elder bathed himself next to the pool.

While bathing, the Elder said, *Wolf, ah wolf, today you let me have some water, but tomorrow where am I going to find you a bowl of corn? I'll catch you a few rats, because I know you like to eat meat.* The Elder thought, *I'm old and weak, and therefore have no choice but to accede to you. However, if this were a decade ago, or even just a few years ago, not only would I not give you any rats to eat, it would be the ultimate act of compassion and mercy for me to simply permit you to pass under my carrying pole.* As the Elder mumbled, he continued washing himself until the clear pool was completely muddy. Then he urinated next to the pool, as the thin layer of sunlight on the top of the cliff gradually dissipated.

After picking two clumps of grass and scattering them over the water in the buckets, the Elder began slowly walking toward the opening of the gully. The buckets tugged the ends of the carrying pole until it was bent like a bow. The pole shuddered every time he took a step, but the grass he had placed in the buckets kept the water from spilling out. The pole produced a moaning sound that echoed through the gully. The Elder thought, *I really am old and should walk slowly. As long as I can make it up to the ridge before nightfall, I will have nothing to fear. The moonlight can escort me back to the hill, and after I pour the water on the cornstalk, the dry spots on its leaves will stop expanding.*

What the Elder hadn't anticipated was that a pack of wolves had already trapped him in the gully.

The original wolf was now in front, leading the way, and when the wolves saw the Elder emerging from the gully, they stopped for a moment. As the wolves were standing there, the lead wolf glanced back, then fearlessly led the others in the direction of the Elder.

The Elder's body exploded in terror, as he realized he had fallen into a trap. He thought, *If only I hadn't taken that bath.* He thought, *If only I hadn't sat down by the side of the pool to rest.* He thought, *If only I had hurried, I would be up on the ridge by now, and the wolves would have had to go away empty-handed.* He nevertheless remained calm. He carefully placed his buckets on the ground and slowly unlatched the carrying pole, then, still holding the pole, headed straight toward the pack of wolves as though he hadn't even seen them. He walked deliberately, and the carrying pole's hooks swung rhythmically back and forth. The wolves approached him, but he continued walking in their direction. The twenty-odd paces that separated them were cut to a dozen, but the Elder calmly continued forward as though he intended to march right into the wolf pack.

The wolves were disconcerted by the Elder's calmness, and they stood motionless in the opening of the gully.

The Elder continued walking straight ahead.

The two wolves at the front of the pack took a couple of steps backward, and as they did so the Elder regained a bit of confidence. He began walking quickly and vigorously, his footsteps so loud that the sound knocked some sand and pebbles down from the side of the cliff. The wolves stared at him, as the Elder proceeded to a part of the gully that was narrow like the opening of a bottle, where he squinted up at the cliff walls on either side. He selected this narrow area to make his stand. He knew the wolves would not be able to come through here, and neither would they be able to circle around and surround him.

The Elder and the wolves faced one another.

The Elder thought, *I just need to stand here and make sure I don't topple over. If I manage this, I may be able to survive long enough to make it out alive.* The sun's final rays disappeared and as night fell, the color of the gully became identical to that of the wolves' fur. In the quiet dusk, a tiny sound began to rise from the bottom of the gully. The Elder counted nine wolves in all, including three large ones, four that were about the same size as the blind dog, and two that appeared to be cubs.

The Elder stood as motionless as a tree.

The wolves' glittering green eyes appeared to be suspended in midair. The deathly silence pressed down on the Elder and the pack of wolves like the darkening mountain ridge. The Elder didn't move, nor did he make a sound. Upon realizing that the reason the Elder had been walking so quickly was to block this portion of the gully, one of the wolves began to howl, and the entire pack began advancing toward him.

The Elder planted his carrying pole in the ground in front of him.

The wolves came to a stop.

The Elder and the wolves were about seven or eight paces from one another. In the final rays of the setting sun, the Elder saw one of the three old wolves standing in the middle of the pack. Its left ear had a large chunk bitten out of it, and its leg appeared crippled. The Elder stared at the old wolf, and the two of them faced each other, until finally the wolf began to howl, at which point the entire pack once again began to advance toward the Elder, as the lead wolf fell to the back of the pack. When the wolves were still five or six paces away, the Elder waved his pole. His grip tightened as he aimed for the middle of the pack – directly at the old wolf's head.

The wolves suddenly came to a halt.

The Elder stared at the lead wolf, as the sun's dying rays swept over the pack. He noticed that the brightest eyes belonged not to the three older wolves, nor to the four midsize ones, but rather to the two cubs. Their gazes were piercingly bright, resembling a layer of water under the sunlight – though beneath this sunlit water there was a layer of fear and confusion. The other wolves kept turning around to look at the lead wolf, who produced a series of bright roars that only they could understand. The setting sun's final rays disappeared, as a sheet of darkness fell over the wolves. In the dark, the wolves' eyes shimmered like light in a blue pond. A foul odor surged through the opening of the gully. This stench was different from the sticky rat stench, in that it was smoother but also extremely clear. It occurred to the Elder that the cornstalk's dry spots probably already covered the entirety of each leaf, and might even have spread to the plant's stem. He reflected, *As long as the dry spots don't reach the center of the stalk and the top remains green, the plant can still be saved.* As the Elder was thinking this, he again heard the lead wolf's piercing howl. His body began to tremble, and he vigorously blinked his eyes. He said to himself, *Apart from this pack of wolves, you mustn't think about anything else. If you keep getting distracted, you will surely die.* Fortunately, the wolves hadn't noticed that the Elder's attention had strayed. As the wolves were about to advance following the lead wolf's howl, the Elder waved his carrying pole. The pole struck the sides of the gully, and as the cold sound wafted over, the wolves began to retreat.

A deadlock hung over the Elder and the wolves like a suspension bridge, and each time they blinked it would sway back and forth in a terrifying manner. The Elder could not see where exactly the wolves' bodies were, so instead he stared at the wolves' green eyes, and each time the eyes moved, he would swing his pole and force them to retreat. Time was like a silent ox pulling a cart, slowly crushing the Elder's will. The moon emerged, and was as round as the wolves' eyes. The Elder felt as though an earthworm were crawling down his back. He knew that his back was covered in sweat, and felt the aching in his legs penetrate his body like daggers. His energy was sapped more by the current deadlock than by his previous exertions. He hoped that the wolves would grow tired of standing there and instead would lie down, or at least move around a bit. Instead, they continued standing motionless in a semicircle five or six paces from the Elder, staring at him intently, like weathered rocks. The Elder could even hear the soft creaking sound of their eyes shifting back and forth, and could see that the fur on their backs had a tint of fire as it rustled in the breeze. The Elder wondered, *Can I outlast them?* He told himself, *You must outlast them, even if it kills you!* The Elder thought, *Each of them has four legs*, *but you only have two, and furthermore are an old man in your seventies.* The Elder said, *My God, night has only just fallen, yet your body is already so cramped up. Surely you don't want to deliver yourself into the wolves' jaws!* One of the cubs couldn't stand still any longer, and when the lead wolf wasn't looking, it lay down, after which the other cub lay down as well. The lead wolf looked at the two cubs, and emitted a purplish-red roar. The cubs bowed their heads and made yelps like blades of green grass. Then, the pack fell silent. The weariness began with the cubs, but after they lay down the Elder seemed to become infected by their exhaustion, and his own legs turned to rubber. He wanted to move, but in the end he merely tensed his tendons and shifted his knee caps, then stood straight again. He couldn't afford to let the older wolves see that he could barely remain upright. He thought, *If you reveal just a bit of exhaustion, they will immediately attack. If you can manage to stand here without moving a muscle, you may live, but if you start to sway, you'll surely die.* The moon, partially occluded by clouds, moved across the sky from east to west. He smelled the clouds' parched scent, and realized that the next day there would again be clear skies. If he were to weigh the sunlight on the mountain top, it would weigh at least five or six *qian*. The Elder glanced up, and saw that there was a dense cloud in front of the moon, and he thought, *Once the moon reaches the cloud, the cloud's shadow will pass over the gully.* Like a sturdy tree, he waited until the shadow passed overhead, and as soon as it covered him like a silk sheet, he took the opportunity to quietly stretch both legs in succession. He instantly felt the *qi* passages in his legs and his upper body connect, as a burst of vital energy surged to his knees. He straightened his body, and the carrying pole hooks produced a sound like that of wet paper ripping. At that instant, the same shadow passed over the wolf pack, and the Elder saw the mass of green eyes move toward him like a swarm of fireflies. He roared, and furiously swung the carrying pole hooks against the sides of the cliff. Rocks and sand fell to the ground beside his feet, like water cascading down. He waited for the sound to subside, as clouds drifted past the opening of the gully. He saw that five of the wolves were now standing only four or five paces from him. Fortunately, he had been able to stretch as the cloud's shadow was passing overhead, and consequently he was now able to make a loud movement, halting the wolves' advance and permitting the stalemate to continue deep into the night.

He thought, *I'm already seventy-two years old, and have endured countless more hardships than you.*

He thought, *As long as I'm in the opening of this gully, surely they won't dare come any nearer.*

He thought, *How can wolves be afraid of a man standing here motionless?*

He said to himself, *You absolutely mustn't doze off – because if you do, you're doomed. Blindy and the cornstalk are both depending on you.*

The two cubs lying on the ground both had their eyes closed. The Elder saw that the brightest two pairs of green eyes were extinguished like lanterns. He discreetly moved his right hand forward on the pole, and when his right hand reached his left, he pinched his left wrist.

He felt the pain surge from his wrist to his eyelids, and his fatigue shuddered as though it had just been seared by a flame. The fatigue dripped from his eyelids into the moonlit gully, and only then did he move his hand back. Another wolf lay down, and its eyelids immediately covered that bright green light. The lead wolf snorted, and the other wolf opened its eyes again.

In the middle of the night, the time began to sound green and luxuriant. Overhead, several stars seemed to be missing and the moonlight had a kind of tragic coolness. The Elder blinked several more times. He discreetly raised one foot and used it to step on his other one, and only then did he feel his eyelids begin to soften. Looking at that moon and stars above, he felt he had managed to make it through more than half the night. The second half was already approaching, like a distant bell tolling the hours. At this point, as long as he could manage to keep standing there without a sound, his drowsiness might be transmitted to the wolves themselves.

Like dampness, this drowsiness did in fact begin to overcome both the Elder and the wolves. Three more wolves lay down. The lead wolf snorted again, but couldn't stop the others, until eventually the lead wolf was the only one left standing. Upon seeing that the original array of green eyes had been reduced to only two, the Elder felt somewhat relieved, and thought to himself, *If only the lead wolf would lie down as well. As soon as it does, I'll be able to quietly stretch my arms and legs.* But not only did the final wolf not lie down, it instead came up to the front of the pack. Thinking that the wolf was trying to cut off his only means of retreat, the Elder suddenly found his back covered in cold sweat. He furiously swung his pole, but between swings the wolf came to a halt, stared, then walked in a semicircle in front of him, before finally withdrawing to where the other wolves were lying on the ground. Then, the lead wolf lay down and closed its eyes as well.

All of the green lanterns were now extinguished.

The Elder sighed. His legs felt weak, but just as he was about to collapse his heart began to pound and he stood up straight again. At that instant, he noticed that the lead wolf was peeking through its half-closed eyes, then closed them again. The Elder didn't sleep, convinced that the lead wolf was simply waiting for him to doze off. He picked up a long vine, removed his belt, and unfastened the carrying pole's two cords. Then he tied them all together to form a long rope. As he was doing this, the Elder deliberately made a loud racket. He noticed that four wolf eyes were watching him, then they closed again.

This time the wolves had really fallen asleep.

Under the soft white moonlight, the nine sleeping wolves resembled a field of freshly turned earth, and a stench emanated from this uneven ground. The Elder removed his shoes and, holding his breath, tiptoed forward a couple of steps. He tied one end of the rope across the opening of the gully, then took a couple of steps back and tied the other end around his own wrist. Finally, he leaned the carrying pole against the sides of the gully, and closed his eyes.

The Elder went to sleep.

The Elder slept as sweetly as fragrant grass, and time swept through his dreams like a whirlwind. Whenever the Elder felt a tug on his wrist, his dreams would be violently interrupted. He would open his eyes, pick up the carrying pole, and point it at the wolves.

The sky finally began to brighten, and the moon and stars quietly disappeared from sight. In the entrance to the gully there was a layer of dark blue. The Elder blinked, and saw that the wolves had broken the portion of the makeshift rope that he had placed several paces in front of him, though the belt portion of the rope was still blocking their escape. The wolves knew that the sound had woken the Elder, so they stood there uneasily, carefully watching both the Elder and his snakelike red belt. As the Elder gripped the carrying pole, he felt a shooting pain, then pointed one end of the pole at the center of the wolf pack. He saw that there were still five wolves in front, but didn't know where the other four had gone. The lead wolf was no longer in front of him either. The Elder blanched but continued staring straight ahead, though his heart was pounding loud enough to knock down houses and buildings. He knew that if even one of those four missing wolves managed to sneak up behind him, this night's deadlock would be shattered and he would die.

The Elder listened intently.

The cold sweat soaked the bottoms of his shoes, and he felt as though he were standing in two pools of cold water. The Elder struggled to determine where the lead wolf could have led those other three midsize wolves. He looked around the opening of the gully and saw a sheen of golden sunlight. He realized that the sun had finally come out. Wolves are nocturnal creatures that cannot tolerate sunlight, and if on that day the sun was as blindingly hot as it had been, these wolves would surely retreat before it reached its full strength. As the Elder was thinking this, he noticed the smell of urine. He was about to see which wolf was the source, when he was distracted by clumps of earth falling on his head from the cliff above.

The Elder and the wolves simultaneously looked up at the top of the cliff, where the Elder saw that the lead wolf was leading a cub toward the entrance of the gully. The Elder then glanced over at the other side of the gully, where he saw another pair of half-grown wolves heading down toward the base of the hill. The old man suddenly realized that while he was sleeping, those four wolves had separated from the main group and proceeded to the top of the cliff, to find a way down to the gully behind him. Unfortunately for the wolves, the gully was too narrow and the cliffs were as steep as walls, and in the end they had no choice but to return in the direction from which they had come. The Elder felt secretly pleased, and his body began to radiate strength like the sun. At this point, the sunlight began to stream into the gully, and up on the cliff the lead wolf howled in frustration. When the five wolves standing in front of the Elder heard this howl, they looked up and examined the Elder and his pole, then turned and headed back toward the entrance of the gully.

The pack retreated.

After maintaining the deadlock for an entire night, the wolf pack finally retreated. As the wolves walked away, they periodically glanced back at the Elder. The Elder was still holding his pole as he watched the wolves retreat. When they reached the entrance, they all turned and stared at him for a moment, then left the gully. Their footsteps gradually faded away, until the sound died out altogether, like autumn leaves falling to the ground. The Elder released his grip and finally dropped the carrying pole. He suddenly felt as though there were bugs crawling up his legs. He looked down, and realized that the urine he had smelled had not been from the wolves, but rather had been his own.

He had been so terrified that he had wet himself without realizing it.

The Elder slapped and cursed the object dangling between his legs, then sat and rested for a while. Seeing that the sunlight was growing brighter, he got up and grabbed the carrying pole, then headed toward the opening of the gully. He found an elevated area, then looked around to confirm that the wolves had, in fact, left. Only then did he place the carrying pole on his shoulders again and walk out with the two buckets.

After the Elder emerged from the gully, he went toward the mountain ridge to the west. Afraid that the wolves would return and realizing he still had a long way to go, he only rested for a moment before proceeding up the path to the mountains. The undulating path was still reddish-brown, and in the sunlight it resembled the backs of a herd of cattle. The Elder placed the buckets of water on the ground and took a breath, then watched the wolves climb a hill in the distance, heading toward the Balou Mountains.

The Elder said, *Damn, did they want to fight me? Do they even know who I am? I am the Elder! I don't care if they are nine wolves — even if they were nine jackals, what would they be able to do to me?*

The Elder gazed in the direction where the wolves had disappeared, and shouted, *Don't fucking leave! Stay here with me for another day or two.* Then he lowered his voice and added, *Yes, go ahead and leave. This spring is mine — it belongs to me, Blindy, and the cornstalk.* The Elder remembered the stalk and its dry spots, and shuddered. He leaned over one of the buckets and drank until his belly was swollen with water, and he no longer felt thirsty or hungry. Then he picked up the buckets and proceeded along the mountain road.

By the time he got back to his field, it was already noon. After having spent an entire day and night looking for water and caught in the standoff with the wolves, the Elder felt as though he was now over a hundred. His beard had been thin and sparse, but overnight it seemed to have grown much longer. By the time he reached Baliban Hill, he was about to topple over like a rootless tree. As he was resting by the side of the road, the blind dog came to him. He noticed that the dog's tongue was cracked, yet its eye sockets were filled with pools of dark water. The dog wept. It had heard the old man's weak footsteps, had

77

smelled the scent of fresh water, and then had staggered up the ridge toward him. When the dog was a few paces away from the Elder, however, it suddenly collapsed.

You need to come here, the Elder said to the dog. *I'm too tired to move.*

The dog crawled forward a couple of paces, then became as still as death. Only its eye sockets continued to well up with tears.

I know you're hungry and thirsty, the Elder said. *It's hard enough just to survive.*

Without a sound, the dog faced the Elder.

The Elder shuddered, and he asked whether the cornstalk had died. The blind dog lowered its head, its tears dripping to the ground.

Leaving the buckets at the top of the ridge, the Elder headed toward the stalk. He kicked up a cloud of dust as he staggered along, and when he reached the shed, his heart began pounding loudly. Under the sun's searing rays, the stalk's leaves didn't have a trace of green left. Even the ribs of the leaves, which had previously been light green, were now dark brown. *That does it,* the Elder thought, regretting that he had not been able to bring the water in time to save the stalk. *It was not you who defeated that pack of wolves, but rather it is they who defeated you. They must have known that the cornstalk had died, which is why they finally decided to leave. It turns out that they were not trying to devour you, but rather they held you up for an entire night precisely in order to ensure the death of this stalk.* Just as he was about to collapse, he looked at the tip of the stalk and saw that in the center of a circle of dry leaves there was a drop of green that struck his gaze with a thump.

The stalk was still alive, and even under the blazing sun it retained a trace of green. The Elder turned over one of the leaves, and saw that on the back there was a thin silklike layer of green, and a starlike array of green dots were visible in the areas between the dry spots. The leaf's ribs were like a bent bow, and there was a trace of steam slowly emanating from it.

The Elder returned to the top of the ridge, where he grabbed a bowl and used it to ladle out some water. Then he placed the water in front of the blind dog's mouth, and said, *The cornstalk is still alive, so leave me this bowl after you finish.* Then the Elder carried a bucket of water to the stalk. He leaned over the bucket and took a mouthful of water, pulled open the top of the cornstalk, then spit out the water. Immediately, a green bead appeared under the searing sun, and as the droplets the Elder spit out landed on the red-hot sunlit area, they produced a sizzling sound. The sunlight devoured the drops before they fell to the ground. The Elder spat seven mouthfuls of water onto the tip of the cornstalk, washing it as clean as though it had rained continuously for seven days and seven nights. After some of the green areas began to regain their original color, the Elder placed the bucket beneath the stalk, and used the bowl to ladle out water and carefully washed each of the leaves. As he did so, he used the bowl to catch the excess water, then poured it back into the bucket. The sound of dripping echoed through the thick sunrays. He washed one leaf after another, and by the time he was on the fourth leaf he saw the blind dog returning from the ridge with a bowl in its mouth. The dog placed the bowl by the shed, then walked over and stood next to the Elder's leg. The Elder asked, *Are you thirsty? There is a spring and plenty of water for you to drink.* The blind dog shook its head, then ran its paws over the surface of the leaves.

The Elder said, *These leaves are still alive. You can relax.*

Standing next to the Elder's legs, the blind dog let out a long sigh, then lay down. It had a gentle and relaxed expression.

As the Elder was going to fetch more water from the pond, he noticed that behind the blind dog there was a black mass resembling a rotten eggplant. When he went to look closely, he saw that the black mass had a reddish tint, and when he tried to kick it, he discovered that it was actually a dead rat. He turned around and saw that there were several more rats inside the enclosure, and when he went back outside he discovered that there were seven or eight more rats lying around, and each of them had red splotches and what looked like bite marks. Obviously, the blind dog had killed them. The Elder called over the blind dog and asked it whether or not this was true. The dog took the Elder's hand in its mouth and pulled him over to the roots of the cornstalk. The Elder saw that rats had gnawed on the stalk's roots, and sap was seeping out. Illuminated by the sun's rays, the sap resembled a bluish-yellow blob. The Elder sat down in front of the stalk's wound and caressed the ball of dried sap, then he patted the dog's head, and said, *Blindy, I'm very grateful to you. In the next life, if I become reincarnated as an animal, I want to become reincarnated as you. And if you become reincarnated as a human, I'd like for you to be reincarnated as my child, and live peacefully your entire life*. At this point, the blind dog's eye sockets filled with tears again. The Elder wiped away the tears, then brought another bowl of water and placed it in front of the dog's mouth, saying, *Go ahead and drink as much as you want. When I go fetch more water, you'll need to stand guard beside the cornstalk*.

The cornstalk was finally revived. For three days in a row, the Elder used buckets of water to irrigate the stalk, and on the morning of the fourth day, he saw that the tip of the stalk was green again. The green color from the back of every leaf had seeped through to the front, and was rapidly expanding like a drop of water on a sheet of straw paper. As the green areas expanded, the dry spots shrank. After several more days, when the Elder gazed at the stalk from the road, he could once again see the green leaves swaying back and forth in the sunlight.

The Elder and the blind dog proceeded to eat the remaining food, but eventually even the days when they could have half a bowl of broth came to an end. The first day that they didn't have anything to eat, the Elder still hauled two buckets half-full of water back from the spring. When he went to fetch more the next day, his sight grew blurry and he began to stumble as soon as he reached the ridge. The Elder knew he couldn't fetch anymore water, so he returned from the ridge and drank until his belly was full. On the third day, the old man was leaning against one of the shed posts watching the sun rise, and he saw that the moon had not yet set, even as the sun's piercing rays were shining down on the ground. He hugged the blind dog, and said, *Go to sleep, Blindy. After you fall asleep, you can sate your hunger in your dreams.* The dog, however, was unable to fall asleep. The sun was shining brightly on the Elder's face and began to produce a burning smell, whereupon he drank another half a bowl of water to sate his hunger, and then he developed an urge to relieve himself. After peeing, he became even more famished than before, so he drank several more times, until there was only a single bowl of water left in the bucket.

The Elder said, *I can't drink anymore. That last bowl is for the cornstalk.*

The sunlight bore down on his head, and the sun's rays now weighed five *qian*.

The Elder said, *Fuck your ancestors, you blasted sunlight.*

The sun's rays now weighed five and a half *qian*, as the sun continued to bear down on his head.

The Elder said, *Can we continue to endure it, Blindy?*

The sun's rays now weighed almost six *qian*. The Elder went to rub the blind dog's belly, which was as soft as a mound of mud.

The Elder said, *You're even skinnier than I am. I've truly failed you, Blindy!*

He touched his own belly, and found that the skin was as thin as a sheet of paper.

The Elder said, *Blindy, you must sleep for a while. After you wake up, there will be something to eat.*

Without saying a word, the dog lay down at the old man's feet. Every hair on its body was long and thin, like sticks and twigs, and the tips of every strand were frayed. The Elder wanted to sleep, but every time he closed his eyes he would hear a rumbling in his belly. He endured this acute hunger for another day, and when the sun once again approached the western mountains, he finally fell asleep. When he reopened his eyes, he had a bright smile on his face. Leaning on one of the shed posts, he stood up and gazed at the setting sun. After estimating that the sun's rays now weighed less than four *qian,* he asked the sun, *Do you think you can outlast me? Who am I? I'm your Elder, that's who!*

The Elder peed a drop of urine in the direction of the setting sun, then said to the dog lying at his feet, *Get up. I told you when you woke up there would be food to eat.*

The blind dog struggled to stand. Its fur was disheveled and matted, and it gave off a brown, burning odor.

The Elder said, *Can you guess what we're going to eat?*

The blind dog faced the old man, a look of disappointment on its face.

The Elder said, *I'll tell you. We're going to have some meat.*

The dog continued to face the old man, staring blankly at him with its blind eyes.

The Elder said, *Really, we are going to have some meat.*

After the Elder said this, the sun cackled with laughter, then sunk below the mountains. In the blink of an eye, the searing heat dissipated, and a cool silklike breeze began blowing over the ridge. The Elder fetched a spade from beside the stove, then went to dig a hole at the end of the field. He dug a large, round pit, as though he were going to plant a tree. The pit was one and a half feet deep, and the edges were as smooth as a cliff. Then he lit a fire and boiled some water. He picked a tassel from the cornstalk, mixed it with the water, and ladled it out, pouring it into the pit. By this point, it was almost dusk, and the mountain ridge was so quiet you could even hear the footsteps of the approaching night. There was damp coolness emanating from the bottom of the gully, and it surrounded the old man and the dog like mist. They sat down in the shed and listened for any movement in the pit, waiting for the night's inky darkness to cover the field.

The Elder asked, *Do you think the rats will fall into the pit?*

The blind dog pressed its ear to the ground and listened carefully.

The moon shone onto the ground, and the ground along the mountain ridge was bathed in watery moonlight. In the silence, the blind dog did indeed hear the rats kicking the moonlight. The Elder quietly felt his way toward the pit, and found that inside there were three rats fighting for food. He quickly covered the pit with a sheet, as the rats stared up in astonishment.

That night, the Elder and the dog caught thirteen rats, and in the light of the moon they skinned, cooked and ate them, as a fragrant stench wafted in all directions. They went to sleep just before daybreak, and woke when the sun was three rod-lengths high in the sky. The Elder tossed the rat pelts into the gully, then hauled the bucket to the pool forty *li* away.

From that day on, there was a period during which the Elder and the blind dog enjoyed a peaceful and uneventful existence. They dug several bottle-shaped pits – each with a narrow opening, a wide base and smooth walls, such that after the rats fell in they wouldn't be able to crawl back out again. Every night, the Elder and the blind dog would bring back a dozen or so corn seeds from the fields, which they would grind and boil until a golden fragrance wafted in all directions. Then, they would pour the broth into the pits and retire to the cool shed to sleep. Sure enough, the next day there would be several rats – sometimes even a dozen or more – trapped in the hole and crying in terror, which would provide the Elder and the blind dog with enough sustenance for another day or two. Every other day the Elder would go to the pool to fetch more water, and in this way their schedule became as smooth as a river without any waves or ripples. About half a month after the crisis, the cornstalk, still alive within the enclosure, produced a thumb-sized bud of an ear. Finally able to relax, the Elder would sit in front of the ear and speak to the blind dog. Once he said, *Blindy, do you think tomorrow this ear will become as large as a rolling pin?* Seeing that the Elder was happy, the blind dog licked his leg. The Elder patted the dog's back, and remarked that normally a cornstalk needed a month and ten days from the time the ear first appeared until it was ready for harvest, so how could this one possibly mature overnight? Another time he said, *Look, isn't this ear already as thick as a finger?* The blind dog went to look at the ear, and the Elder said, *You're blind. How can you see? This ear is already thicker than my thumb.*

One day, the Elder returned with water, and after irrigating the cornstalk he proceeded to hoe part of the field, whereupon he noticed that the ear had already started producing milky-white silk that resembled an infant's fuzzy hair. The Elder stood in front of the ear and stared in amazement, then laughed and said, *It's almost ready for harvest. Blindy, do you see that? It's almost ready for harvest!*

Hearing no response, the Elder turned and saw that the blind dog was next to the gully eating the previous day's leftover rat pelts. There was a horrendous stench, and the ground was covered in rat fur. The Elder exclaimed, *Blindy, isn't that filthy?* The blind dog didn't respond, and instead headed toward the pit. The Elder followed the dog to the edge of the pit, and his heart began pounding as he saw that this time there was only a single rat inside. This was his smallest yield since he began trapping rats half a month earlier. The previous day there had been four rats, and the day before that there had been five. But now there was only one. The Elder proceeded to dig several more pits along other ridges, and in each he placed several corn tassels, but the following day half of the pits were still empty and the remainder had only one or two rats each.

Never again did the Elder enjoy the good fortune of having a dozen or more rats fall into a single pit, and consequently the days of abundant food and water had come to an end. The Elder went up the mountain ridge and, after using the scale to weigh the sunlight, he stood there facing the sharp light, as a feeling of terror welled up inside him. This feeling started as a single bud but quickly grew into a vast forest covering the entire mountainside.

The Elder collected a rat from one of the pits and took it back to skin and cook, then wrapped it in cloth. Next, he patted the blind dog's head and told it to guard the field while he was away. The Elder departed, and after walking aimlessly for a while, he passed five villages and finally reached the tallest peak in the area. He stopped and faced the sun, then took out his scale and weighed the sunlight. He sighed, sat down, and rested in the shade at the base of a cliff. The cliff was as steep as a wall, and clumps of dirt periodically fell from the top. The Elder saw that the fields in front of him were so dry and cracked that they looked as though a net had been thrown over them. He peered farther into the distance, and saw that the serpentine mountain ridge resembled an endless series of bonfires. After staring for a while, his eyes began to ache from the heat. He took a cloth bundle from his pocket, unwrapped it, and removed the dead rat. When he had initially cooked the rat, the meat had been bright red, but after only half a day it had turned as black as sludge. The Elder sniffed it, but found that its original fragrance had disappeared and all that remained was a foul gray odor and a faint moldy smell. However, after having spent all day walking through the mountains, he was absolutely famished. He tore off one of the rat's legs and was about to eat it, when he noticed that there were several tiny white objects moving around in the meat. He shuddered and was about to throw the meat away, but changed his mind.

The Elder closed his eyes, opened his mouth, and stuffed the rat inside. He bit off two-thirds of it, chewed vigorously, and swallowed the entire thing in two bites.

When the Elder opened his eyes, he saw that on the ground in front of him there were a couple of maggots, which instantly dried up.

As dusk fell, the Elder returned to his field and proceeded to sit beside the cornstalk all night without sleeping. Regardless of how much the blind dog tried to cozy up to him, the Elder remained unresponsive. He gazed at the sky, then looked at the corn ear that was in the process of turning red. Finally, after the sun rose, the Elder suddenly got up and headed back to the village.

The mountains appeared vast and silent. The blind dog followed the Elder for a few steps, then went back to stand guard by the cornstalk.

The dog waited for the Elder to return.

At midday, the Elder returned. He had rolled a large brown barrel back from the village, and positioned it next to the cornstalk. Then he went up the ridge to catch a large rat. Holding the rat by the neck, he took it to the shed and killed it with a cleaver, collecting the blood in a bowl. He fed the pelt to the blind dog, while he stewed the blood and cooked the meat. He drank the stewed blood, then wrapped up the meat, collected his buckets, and headed out.

The Elder wanted to bring back enough water to fill up the entire barrel.

The Elder calculated that there were a total of nine rats left in the thirty pits he had dug. Given that he and the blind dog would need to eat at least one rat a day to avoid starvation, that meant they would run out of food in nine days. Of all the corn seeds the villagers had planted a few months earlier, there was nothing left. The harvest season was approaching and the sunlight was becoming progressively heavier, and this was precisely when the cornstalk most needed water and nutrients. The Elder decided he had to fill the barrel within the next nine days, so that even if he and the blind dog died, the cornstalk would still have sufficient water and nutrients to produce an ear of corn. The Elder walked over from the mountain road, as one bundle of sunlight after another beat down on his body. He again smelled the stench of burning fur, so he put the rat in the bucket and covered it with his straw hat. He wiped the sweat pouring down his forehead with his finger, then licked it. He felt sweat dripping onto his knee, so he squatted down and sucked that, too. He did everything he could to prevent his sweat from evaporating in the sunlight. The good thing was that every morning before dawn he would take his buckets and proceed north, and by the time the sun came up and sweat started pouring from his body, he would be within five or six *li* of the pool, and therefore it would only be during these final five or six *li* that he would have to resort to drinking his own sweat. By the time the sun was directly overhead, he would have reached the pool, where he would drink until his belly was full, eat the rat meat, then carry a couple of buckets of water up the hill. On the way back, when he was thirsty, he would drink directly out of one of the buckets. At this point, the sunlight would weigh eight or nine *qian*. He would periodically hear the sound of his sweat pouring down. He didn't hate the sunlight, nor did he resent the drought, but as his legs were trembling he would ask himself, *Am I old now? In the village, there have been men in their seventies who were still able to father a child, so why can't I manage to carry a couple of buckets of water?* His legs were trembling uncontrollably, so he had no alternative but to put down the buckets to rest for a while. He leaned over one of the buckets and drank until his belly was engorged. The Elder calculated that every time he went to fetch some water, he would have to stop and rest at least twenty or thirty times over the course of the forty-*li* trip. Furthermore, every time he stopped to rest, he would drink some water. As a result, he would drink, then sweat, then drink some more. But regardless of how often he stopped to rest and how much water he drank, by the time he got back to the field, the two buckets of water he had fetched from the pool would inevitably have been reduced to one.

After five days, the barrel was only one-third full, but the Elder had already consumed five rats. The remaining four would be his food for the next four days. In the sunlight, the stalk turned dark green, but after the tassel began to turn red, the stalk paused to rest. The new ear was as long and thick as a daikon, but the silk still refused to turn black, and the tassel also refused to have even a trace of yellow. With the tassel not turning yellow and the silk not turning black, it seemed as though the corn had a long way to go before it was ripe. At dusk, when the mountains appeared bathed in blood, the Elder would stroke the corn's green ear. Its softness would give him a chill, as he wondered when it would ever ripen. Based on the stalk's growth rate, it would need at least another twenty or thirty days. He calculated that it had already been at least four months since the other villagers departed. Corn normally needed about four and a half months to ripen, but the repeated delays in this stalk's ripening filled the Elder's forehead with furrows of anxiety. He led the blind dog out to the pits he had dug, but they didn't find a single rodent inside. Facing the mountain ridge, the Elder lay down on the side of the road. The ground beneath him was burning hot, and the heat passed through his back and circulated through his body. The blind dog lay down beside him – so emaciated that it didn't seem to have the energy to get up again. There was a rat squeaking from hunger, and when the faint sound made its way to them from the pit, it aroused a seismic hunger in the Elder and the blind dog.

The blind dog stared in the direction of the rat's cries.

The Elder gazed up at the sky, as silent as the ages.

Later, the Elder rolled over and began making a loud movement. The blind dog assumed the Elder was finally going to say something, and quickly turned in his direction. The Elder, however, merely stood up and walked away without saying a word. He felt the corn ear's firmness, mumbled something incoherent, and then, in the light of the moon, grabbed the buckets and headed north.

That night, the Elder brought back another load of water. This time he didn't drink a single drop, and instead returned with two full buckets. He poured one and a half buckets into the barrel. From the remaining half bucket, he used several bowls to irrigate the corn-stalk, and poured another several bowls into a basin, so that the blind dog could drink from it whenever it was thirsty. Afterward, he cooked several rats, collected his buckets, and headed off again.

Over the next three days, the Elder brought back a full load of water every night and half a load of water every day – until the barrel was full.

The Elder decided that since he retained a bit of strength and there was still a rat in one of the pits, he would go down to the spring to fetch water one last time. This final load of water would be enough to last him and the blind dog for several more days. He wasn't holding out hope that it would rain, but he did hope that he and the blind dog could survive until the corn ripened, and would finally be able to break open this ear of corn. The ear appeared to have about thirty-five seeds in each row, and at least twenty-three rows. That meant that one ear would contain several hundred seeds. Four and a half months had passed, and the harvest season was inexorably drawing nearer. At midday the Elder could already smell the sticky yellow scent of the corn ripening, and by midnight this scent had become as pure as sesame oil.

That night, while the moon was overhead, the Elder set out to fetch the final load of water. By the time he returned, it was already afternoon of the following day. On the road, he stopped to rest forty-one times, and drank an entire bucket of water. He took the remaining bucket to the top of the mountain ridge, where he rested until dusk. He was convinced he didn't have the strength to carry this bucket down to the shed, so instead he decided to cook and eat the remaining rat. That was the largest of the original nine rats – it was one palm long, and its eyes were bright red. But when the Elder reached the pit where the rat had been trapped, he discovered it was full of dog paw prints, rat fur, and blood stains.

The Elder squatted next to that pit until the sky was dark.

When the moon appeared overhead, the Elder finally laughed and, like a sheet of slowly cracking ice, began to speak. He stood up and, gazing out at the smoky shadows moving under the moonlight, remarked, *It's fine for you to eat it, because now that you've done so I can tell you that eventually either you will eat me and then live with the cornstalk, or otherwise I'll eat you.* The Elder thought, *I can finally say this to Blindy. For days, I've been waiting for this opportunity.* The Elder returned to the ridge to fetch the buckets of water he had left there. Although his legs were weak, he was able to slowly proceed forward and collect the water, then carry it down to the shed.

The blind dog was lying under the shed, but it immediately got up when it heard the Elder's footsteps. It seemed to want to walk over to the Elder, but instead retreated a few paces and lay down in the opening to the enclosure. The moon was bright and appeared to be covered with hot gas. The Elder placed the buckets next to the barrel, and removed the mat on top to check the water level. He took off his shoes and shook out the dirt and sand; then, after staring at the whip hanging from one of the shed's support posts, he coughed and said softly, *Blindy, come here.*

This was the first time in days that the blind dog had heard the Elder's voice. The dog struggled to get up and hesitantly took a step forward, then stood still, facing in the direction where the Elder was sitting, its sparse fur making a shivering sound. The Elder looked off into the distance, then said, *Blindy, there's no need to be afraid. If you ate it, that's fine. That was going to be our last bite of food, and I don't mind if you took my portion.* Then the Elder added, *There's one more thing I need to tell you, Blindy. There isn't a single rat or corn seed left in this entire mountain range. Within three days, you and I will be so famished that we won't even have the energy to utter a word. At that point, if you want to survive, you'll need to consume me piece by piece. Then you must guard this cornstalk, so that when the other villagers return, you can lead them over and let them pick the ear of corn. Otherwise, if you appreciate what I have done to support you these past four or five months and want to help me stay alive, you must permit me to consume you, so that I may survive until the corn ripens.* The Elder added, *Blindy, you must decide. If you want to live, then tonight you must leave and hide somewhere. In a few days, I will starve to death.* Upon saying this, the Elder wiped his face, as two rows of tears wet his palm.

The blind dog stood there motionless, waiting for the Elder to finish speaking before taking a few steps toward him. When the dog reached the Elder's knees, it slowly bent its front legs while keeping its rear legs straight. It lifted its skinny head and stared silently at the Elder with eyes that resembled empty wells.

The Elder knew the dog was kneeling before him.

After kneeling down, the dog got back up and slowly walked toward the stove, where it used its mouth to open the pot and retrieve something from inside. Then it returned to the Elder.

The dog brought over the object it had taken out of the pot, and placed it at the Elder's feet. It was a skinned rat, which was soaking wet and appeared purple in the moonlight. The Elder knew at a glance that this rat was still full of blood, unlike the ones the Elder had killed, which bled out when he disemboweled them. The Elder picked up the piece of purple meat and examined it, and found that it was riddled with bite marks. He sighed, and said to the dog, *Why didn't you eat the rat yourself? When I said you could have it, I meant it. There was no need to save it for me.* The Elder suddenly regretted that he had raised the possibility that one of them might have to die in order for the other to survive. He examined the meat in the moonlight, and remarked, *The abdomen is completely purple. The meat probably won't taste as good as it would have had the rat been killed with a knife.*

The blind dog lay down next to the Elder and rested its head on his leg.

The Elder cooked the rat meat the next day, and gave the blind dog half. He said, *Eat it. You need to survive for as long as you can.* The blind dog refused, so the Elder forced the animal's mouth open and stuffed in the rat's head and three of its legs. The Elder then took the remainder and stood in front of the cornstalk, chewing carefully. He knew that after he finished these final two bites, their food supply would truly be exhausted, and he would have no alternative but to starve to death. If he had to die, then so be it. He was seventy-two years old, which was considered elderly in this mountain region. Despite the drought, during which time all the remaining food was consumed, he not only managed to survive another half a year, he even managed to grow this cornstalk that was already three heads taller than he, with long and wide leaves, and an ear as large as a daikon. As the Elder stared intently at the ear's silk, he swallowed the rat meat in a few bites, then put his finger in his mouth and sucked on it noisily. At that moment, something began fluttering down onto his face like snow. The Elder looked up, his finger still in his mouth, and saw that the top of the cornstalk, which had previously been yellowish-white, had turned reddish-black overnight, and tiny chaff-like flakes were now flying everywhere. That is to say, the cornstalk was starting to pollinate and would soon begin producing seeds, meaning that harvest time had almost arrived. The Elder looked at the sky, and saw ray after ray of blindingly white sunshine bumping into one another. *It would be better if there were some wind,* the Elder thought. *At this time of year, it is better if there's some wind. If there were wind, the pollen would be distributed quickly and evenly, and the sprouts would grow evenly and sturdily.* The Elder removed his finger from his mouth and wiped it on his pants. Then, he began carefully pinching the corn ear. Through the thick peel, the Elder could feel that inside the soft ear there was a layer of firm objects. The Elder's heart skipped a beat, as though a door had suddenly slammed shut. His hand remained poised over the ear and he continued to stare into the sky, his mouth tightly closed. A moment later, after confirming that the kernels were firm, it was as if a door had reopened, and a surge of excitement coursed through his body. An excited expression fell across his face, and it appeared as though there were a river flowing beneath his dark, wrinkled skin. His hands began to itch uncontrollably. He blew on them, then walked out of the enclosure, took the hoe that was hanging from the pagoda tree, and began digging around the cornstalk. Dirt rained down, as fine as wheat or millet, and carried a golden scent of autumn harvest. He continued digging around the cornstalk until he reached the reed mats, by which point he was so exhausted that his gasps sounded like a severed rope. He dismantled the enclosure and tossed the mats under the tree. The blind dog followed him, not knowing what else to do. Without a word, the Elder dug past the enclosure's support posts, then turned and dug a perimeter around the barrel. He continued until he accidentally struck the barrel, producing a sharp, moist sound. The Elder stopped and stood there, a bright smile on his face. He said, *Blindy, it's harvest time. The cornstalk has finally produced seeds!*

The blind dog licked its lips.

The Elder lay on the ground and said to the heavens, *The moment I've been waiting for has finally arrived. It's finally harvest time!*

The blind dog licked the Elder's fingers.

While being licked by the blind dog's ticklish tongue, the Elder fell asleep.

After he awoke, the Elder went to see that ear of corn, and the look of excitement immediately vanished from his face. He discovered that the stalk's leaves were not as green as before, and instead a layer of yellow was now showing through. This yellow layer was visible not only on the stalk's lowermost leaves, but also in the leaves that had just sprouted from the top. The Elder had been farming for his entire life, and recognized that this was a sign that the stalk lacked fertilizer. This was the period when the stalk was ready to ripen, but only with sufficient nutrition would it be able to produce all of its seeds. The best fertilizer was human night soil. In the past, the Elder always fertilized his fields with night soil, and consequently his crops – including wheat, beans and sorghum – had always been the best in the village. Indeed, he was, without a doubt, the best farmer in the entire region. Standing in front of his cornstalk, his lips had become as dry as the drought-stricken ground along the mountain ridge, but he didn't go over to drink water, nor did he ladle out any for the blind dog to drink. He didn't know where he should go to find some night soil. The village's outhouses were all so dry they were enveloped in clouds of dust, and any excrement that remained had become so desiccated that it had less value as fertilizer than firewood. The Elder and the blind dog had both gone several days without needing to relieve themselves, since their intestines had absorbed most of the rat meat and bone residue they had managed to eat. The Elder remembered the rat pelts he had eaten, and he went to look for more, but couldn't find a single one. He suspected that the blind dog must have eaten them while he was out fetching water. Panting heavily, he climbed up from the base of the hill. He originally wanted to ask the blind dog about this, but in the end he merely went to the pot that had had the rat and drank a bowl of oily broth. He didn't cover the pot when he was finished, and instead turned and said to the dog, *Whenever you are hungry or thirsty, you should go drink.* Then the Elder took his grain sack and went to the village to look for fertilizer.

When the Elder returned from the village with an empty bag, he was leaning on a bamboo stick, and every three steps he had to stop and rest. Exhausted, he dropped the empty bag to the ground, then went to see the blind dog, who was still lying under the shed. The water in the pot was still as he had left it, and the same eleven drops of oil were still floating on top. He asked the dog, *You didn't drink any?* The dog moved weakly, and the Elder used a spoon to drink half a bowl of water, including five of the eleven drops of oil. Then he said to the blind dog, *The remainder is for you.* He went back to the cornstalk, and when he looked at the leaves he saw that the thin layer of yellow appeared to have grown darker, and the green now appeared to be submerged beneath the yellow. The Elder thought, *Why didn't you prepare some fertilizer earlier? Aren't you the village's Elder? Fuck your ancestors — why didn't it occur to me that the cornstalk would need extra fertilizer when it started to produce seeds?!*

That night, the Elder slept under the cornstalk, and when he woke the next morning he noticed that the green color of several of the leaves had completely faded, and instead the leaves were now covered with a paperlike sheet of yellow.

The following night, the Elder once again slept under the cornstalk, and when he woke the next morning he discovered that not only were two of the leaves completely yellow, but the silk on the ear of corn had prematurely dried out. He pinched the ear, and found it to be as soft as mud. Like the bones in his body, the semihard objects inside the ear had also disappeared.

The third night, the Elder yet again went to the cornstalk, but this time he didn't sleep and instead used the hoe to dig a trench. The resulting trench was half a foot wide, three feet deep, and five feet long – just the right size for someone to lie down, and more than large enough for a dog.

This was a grave.

Given that the grave was positioned right next to the cornstalk, several of the stalk's roots were exposed to it. Once the Elder finished digging, he lay down to rest, then went to the stove to see whether the remaining half-bowl of meat broth – with the six drops of oil – was still in the pot. He wanted to drink some, so he picked up the spoon but immediately put it down again, saying to himself, *This last half-bowl was for the blind dog, but now three days have passed.* He said to the dog, *Blindy, three days have passed. Why haven't you drunk it yet?*

The blind dog was in the shed. It had been lying there motionless for three days, as the cool night air poured over its body. The dog lifted its head and stared, with its blind eyes, in the direction of the Elder's voice. The dog didn't follow the Elder's instructions, and instead merely rested its head on its front legs. By this point, a hazy light had begun to appear in the sky, and the darkness covering the mountain ridge was being replaced with the light of day. The Elder leaned over the barrel and took several sips of water, then took out a pair of scissors and used them to punch a hole in the base of the barrel.

After the Elder punched the hole in the base of the barrel and water started flowing out, he took some dirt and caked it over the opening. Having nothing else to do, he hung his hoe on the tree branch and lay his shovel next to the grave. He placed a mat over the top of the barrel, then folded his quilt inside the shed, gathered up his bowl, chopsticks and spoon, and placed them under the shed post. Finally, he went to the stalk and examined the light yellow color that was gradually spreading over the leaves. He pinched the ear, which resembled a water bag. He turned around as the sun burst out from between two mountain peaks in the east, making the mountains appear as though they were drenched in blood. The Elder stood between the cornstalk and the shed, and gazed at the mountain ridge. It was as if there were thousands upon thousands of cattle running in all directions. He was so exhausted he couldn't even see straight. He rubbed his eyes, glanced up at the sky, and saw an array of scalelike clouds with silver linings hopping around in front of the sun, like countless fish swimming around in a pond. The Elder thought to himself, *Today the sunlight must weigh at least 1.4* liang. He turned and glanced at the scale hanging from the shed post, then edged over to the blind dog. He lifted the dog and placed it in the grave, rubbing its body against the four sides of the grave. Then he removed the dog, and said, *Blindy, either you or I will die, and whichever of us survives must bury the other in this grave.* The Elder stroked the dog's back and wiped the tears from its eyes. He took a coin out of his pocket and placed it heads-up, then rubbed the dog's right paw over it. He said, *Fate will determine whether we live or die. I'll toss this coin, and if it lands heads-up, you must bury me in this grave so that my body may serve as fertilizer; and if it lands heads-down, then I must bury you.*

The dog's well-like eyes stared at the coin in the Elder's hand, as murky blackish-red tears welled up in its eye sockets and dripped down into the newly dug grave.

There's no need to cry, the Elder said. *If after my death I am reincarnated as an animal, I want to be reincarnated as you. And if you are to be reincarnated as a human, you may be reincarnated as my child. That way, we can continue living together.*

The dog's tears stopped flowing. It made an effort to stand up, but its forelegs collapsed and it lay back down inside the grave.

The Elder said, *Go drink the final half-bowl of broth in the pot.*

The blind dog bowed its head toward the Elder.

The Elder said, *I'm going to toss this coin. Whichever of us still has any energy left can bury the other in this grave.*

The blind dog faced the ground.

After brushing the dog's back three more times, the Elder stood up. The sun was marching over toward the mountain ridge, and if you listened carefully you could hear a fire burning brightly in the void. The Elder cursed, *Fuck your ancestors!* He glanced down at the coin one last time, then turned to the dog and said, *I'm going to toss it.* He proceeded to throw the coin into the air. The sun's rays were as dense as trees in a forest, and the coin bumped against one ray after another, producing a bright clinking sound. When the coin landed, it tumbled over and over, slicing those rays of sunlight into countless individual shards. The Elder watched the coin as it fell, as though staring at an enormous raindrop that had suddenly appeared before him. The blind dog stood up as well. It heard the reddish-yellow sound the coin was making as it tumbled through the air, like a ripe apricot falling onto the grass.

The Elder walked over to the coin.

The blind dog followed him.

The Elder reached a clump of earth he had dug up and, without bending over all the way, he stood up again. He sighed, and said calmly, *Blindy, go finish that final half-bowl of broth, which will grant you enough energy to bury me.*

The blind dog stood there without moving.

The Elder said, *Go on. Do what I say. After drinking the broth, you'll have to bury me.*

The dog still didn't leave. Instead, it bent its forelegs and once again bowed down to the Elder. The Elder said, *Blindy, there's no need to bow. It is Heaven's will that I should serve as fertilizer for this cornstalk.* Then, he picked up the coin, patted the dog's head, and said, *If you feel bad about this, I could flip the coin twice more, and if it lands heads-up two times out of three, then I die; and if it lands heads-down two times out of three, then you die.*

The blind dog stood up.

The Elder tossed the coin again, and it landed in front of the blind dog. The Elder took a look, and announced there was no need to toss it again. Then he sat down limply. The blind dog went over to where it had heard the coin fall. It touched the coin with its paw, licked the coin with its tongue, then lay down, as tears streamed down its face. Instantly, two pools of mud accumulated beneath its head.

Go drink that final half-bowl of broth, the Elder said. *Afterward, you can bury me.* Upon saying this, the Elder got up and went over to the shed post, where he pulled out a thin bamboo pole. The hollow pole was more than two feet long, and when you blew on it, it sounded very melodious. He inserted the pole horizontally into the hole he had punched in the base of the water barrel, then sealed the area around it so that no water would leak out. Next he pressed down on the other end of the pole, and a series of jade-like drops of water dripped out of the barrel onto the soil around the cornstalk. Immediately, the soil began to produce a greenish-red sucking sound, leaving behind a large wet area.

The Elder used some loose soil to erect a ring around the base of the cornstalk, to prevent the water from flowing away. After finishing this delicate task, he brushed the dirt from his hands, then looked up at the sun. He took out his scale to weigh the sun's rays, and found that they now weighed 1.5 *liang*. Then he took his whip, stood in an empty area, and whipped the sun more than a dozen times, until shards of light rained down around him like pear blossoms. Finally, exhausted, he hung up the whip, cleared his throat, and announced to the sun, *If I, your Elder, want to continue raising this cornstalk, what are you fucking going to do about it?*

From the sun's rays he heard a hoarse reply, like a broken gong. The sound progressed from this hill to the next one, going farther and farther until it finally disappeared. The Elder waited until the sound had completely faded away, whereupon he rolled up one of the mats and headed toward the grave he had just dug. Then he said to the blind dog, *After burying me, you should go north, following the road I told you about. When you reach the gully with the spring, you will find water, and the ground will be covered with bones left behind by the wolves. You can live there until the drought passes and the villagers return. But I won't be able to make it, given that I'll die either today, tomorrow, or the next day.* The sun was shining on the Elder's forehead, and the bits of dirt in his hair made a clanging sound as they bumped against one another. After the Elder finished speaking to the blind dog, he brushed the dirt from his hair and lay down in the grave, against the side where the roots of the cornstalk were. He covered his body with a mat, then said to the blind dog, *Bury me, Blindy. Bury me, then go north.*

The mountains were silent. The flames hidden in the searing sunlight suddenly became more energetic. In the boundless emptiness, a burning smell began spreading across the entire mountain ridge. The mountains and gullies, villages and roads, and dried-up riverbeds – they were all full of a thick and sticky sunlight that resembled a golden soup.

It was generally assumed that if it didn't rain in autumn, it would definitely snow the following winter. This year, however, winter came late, and it proved to be very dry. The drought continued unabated until the end of the following summer, at which point, rain clouds finally appeared. For half a month, the clouds repeatedly accumulated and dispersed, until finally it began to rain. A darkness then hung over the mountain range for forty-five days, as though the sun had been covered by a shroud. The rain blanketed the earth, flooding the entire land, and by the time the rain stopped and the skies cleared, it was already the autumn sowing season. Villagers gradually began to return to the ridge, bringing back their bedding, dishes and children. At night, their halting footsteps resonated brightly under the moonlight.

During the day, the mountain ridge once again became fully populated, with the jumbled sounds of people pulling carts, carrying loads, and talking; and over the mountain ridge, every now and then, there would be the sound of trees and vegetation coursing down like a river.

By this point, the autumn sowing season had arrived, but the villagers were shocked to discover that their autumn seeds were missing. In fact, there were no seeds at all in the entire several-hundred-square-*li* area of the Balou Mountains.

Suddenly, one of the villagers remembered how the Elder had stayed behind to look after a corn seedling. The villagers rushed out to the Elder's plot of land, and from a distance they could see that in the entire field there was only a solitary shed. When they reached the shed, they saw that the area the Elder had hoed was now full of grass that looked as though it had been planted, producing a thick layer of green that emanated the blue scent of fresh barley and a light white odor. Throughout the entire mountain range, they heard these smells clanking together, the way that on a quiet night one might hear the sound of a river flowing. In this green field, the villagers saw the cornstalk that had already matured the previous year. Its tip had been broken off and its stem was now as thick as a small tree. The stalk was next to two reed mats that were leaning over, and its leaves were covered in mold. Some of the leaves had fallen to the ground, while others were still growing. The stem, meanwhile, looked as though it were covered in paper that had been soaked in water and then dried out again. Hanging from the stalk there was an ear of corn as large as a wooden club used for washing clothes, and it was swaying in the wind. When the ear's jet-black tassels were touched, they would fall to the grass like wilted flower petals. The villagers picked this ear and quickly shucked it, and discovered that inside this enormous ear, which was as thick as a man's calf and as long as an arm, there were thirty-seven rows of corn. But out of those thirty-seven rows, there were only seven fingernail-sized grains that were as bright as pieces of jade, and all the rest had dried up before they had a chance to ripen.

These seven grains of corn were arrayed against a desiccated backdrop, like stars in a night sky. The villagers stared at this ear with only seven grains. They stood silently in the shed looking around, until finally they saw that the mat that had once been on top of the barrel had been blown over to the stove. Inside the barrel there wasn't a single drop of water, merely a thick layer of dirt. The thin bamboo pole that had been inserted into the base of the barrel was already cracked in multiple places. A bowl and spoon were still sitting on one side of the barrel, and a whip and scale were hanging from one of the shed's posts. About five feet from the barrel, on the grass right next to the cornstalk, there was a grassy mound. There was also a trench about half a foot wide, five feet long and three feet deep. A dog was lying in the dense vegetation at one end of the trench, its scraggly body full of maggot holes. Its eye sockets were as empty as dark wells, and its entire body had been dried up by the sun. Gently, the villagers kicked the animal out of the trench as though it were a bundle of kindling, after which the grave-like shape of the trench became obvious. The villagers' hearts pounded, as they realized that this must be the Elder's grave. In order to move the Elder's body to the cemetery, the villagers dug up this pit. With the first shovel, they heard a bright clanking sound, as though they were digging up a metallic joint. They carefully removed the grass from the pit, and turned over the loose earth. Then every villager stared in shock, as they saw that the Elder's underpants had decomposed into soil. His entire body had disintegrated and every joint had come apart. There was a pungent white mist rising like smoke. The Elder was lying in the grave, with one arm in the process of reaching out to the cornstalk while the rest of his body huddled around the base. His corpse was riddled with maggot holes, which were much more numerous than the dog's. Each of the stalk's roots resembled a long and

thin vine, and had a pinkish tint. The roots were growing into the Elder's body through the holes in his chest,
thighs, wrists and abdomen. There were several red roots
as thick as chopsticks growing right through the Elder's
decayed body and into his skull, ribs, and arm and leg
bones. There were several reddish-white tendrils growing
into his eye sockets and poking out through the back of
his skull, gripping the packed earth along the bottom of
the grave. Every joint and every piece of flesh had been
transformed into a web of roots, tightly linking his body
to the cornstalk itself. It was at this point that the villagers
noticed that the cornstalk now had two stems, which had
managed to survive the previous winter and summer and
still retained a trace of green.

After some deliberation, the villagers reburied the
Elder in his original location, and also buried the dog,
which now resembled dried grass, in that grave right next
to him. The smell of fresh earth was mixed with a thin
layer of warm putrefaction. Finally, as the villagers were
about to leave, someone noticed that in the shed, under
the Elder's pillow, there was a rain-soaked calendar. In
the grass outside, someone found a coin covered in rust.
When they wiped away the rust, they noticed that the
coin had text on both sides – meaning that both sides
were 'heads'. No one had ever seen a coin with text on

both sides before. The villagers passed it around, then tossed it into the air. The sun was shining brightly, and in the air the coin collided with one bundle of sunrays after another, producing a sound like red flower petals. The coin fell to the ground, then rolled into a ditch.

The villagers took the calendar back with them.

Eventually, it was harvest season again. After the villagers of the Balou Mountains had finished the food they brought back with them, they had been unable to find any corn seeds to sow, and many of them left in search for food. Within half a month, the entire region was completely depopulated, and in the process became so peaceful you could even hear the bright sound of the sunrays knocking against one another and the moon-beams striking the ground.

In the end, the only people left were seven men from seven of the village's households. They were all young and strong, and proceeded to build seven sheds on seven different mountain ridges. On seven nonadjacent plots of land, under the unremitting sunlight, they planted seven corn seedlings, each of which was as tender as oil.